BOOKS BY HELEN PIERCE JACOB

The Secret of the Strawbridge Place
The Diary of the Strawbridge Place

The Diary of the
Strawbridge Place

The Diary of the

HELEN PIERCE JACOB

Strawbridge Place

Atheneum · New York · 1978

J

J

Library of Congress Cataloging in Publication Data

Jacob, Helen Pierce.
The diary of the Strawbridge place.

SUMMARY: A family of Quakers operating a station
on the Underground Railroad spirits slaves
from Ashtabula, Ohio, across Lake Erie to freedom.
[1. Underground railroad—Fiction.
2. Slavery in the United States—Fiction] I. Title.
PZ7.J139Di [Fic] 77-22713
ISBN 0-689-30619-9

Published simultaneously in Canada by
McClelland & Stewart, Ltd.
Manufactured in the United States of America by
Fairfield Graphics, Fairfield, Pennsylvania
Designed by Mary M. Ahern
First Edition

For Aaron, Kyle, Elliott,
and Papa Clyde who set me straight.

The Diary of the
Strawbridge Place

Chapter 1

It was high noon, and Victory was halfway to the new north field where Homer and Daniel were clearing trees when she heard a gun go off. The heavy water jug and lunch basket pressed against her cotton skirt as she stopped in alarm. Everybody in Ashtabula and the three counties about knew that the Strawbridge farm was out of bounds for hunters and trappers, for the Strawbridges were one of the few Quaker families in the region. Father's property lines were well fenced, and every. . . .

Everybody?

Everybody, Victory suddenly thought, except those laborers the railroad had brought in three months ago to build the new trestle across the Grand River. Forty men, no families with them, sleeping and eating at Blackman's warehouse, drinking at the Blue Moon Saloon, or loafing about Constable Gilly's office hoping for some slave-catching excitement. Ashtabula wanted the trestle, but the village didn't like that rowdy gang.

Victory broke into a run, but her long dark skirt and petticoat snagged on the thorns of a drooping blackberry vine. That Widow Pembroke anyway! She'd let her place go wild since her grandson, Gus, had run off to the gold fields in California two years ago. Father had been trying to persuade the Widow to sell her land since New Year's, and finally, just last week, she'd agreed and accepted his payment in gold for these ten wooded acres that bordered the railroad. Father still had his eye on the rest of the Widow's property, and if and when he got it, the Strawbridge Place would be the largest farm with the best stables and pastureland in the northeastern corner of Ohio.

A second gunshot shattered the spring softness. Victory raced toward the sound. Homer—Daniel—she had to get to them. As she burst out of the thicket of berry bushes, a partially cleared field stretched away to the solid line of trees that bordered the steep riverbank. In the far corner stood the team, Beauty and Molly, heads down, tails switching. They were hitched to a **great** jagged stump, but the reins hung limply along their backs. Her brothers were nowhere in sight.

Victory ran to the team. Beauty welcomed her with a nicker. The jug and basket slipped from her hands as she turned, looking this way and that. The breeze, straight off Lake Erie, brought a shout from the direction of the railroad. Had some of that railroad gang drifted down here to hunt and encountered her brothers? Should she go up there—or should she run home for help? A red-winged blackbird swooped down and disappeared in the direction of the shout. Victory took it for a sign, closed her eyes, prayed fervently, then picked up her gray ankle-length skirts and started toward the shout. If anything happened to Homer or Daniel . . . !

A limb slapped her face and caught in the thick braid

of black hair wound about her head. With fumbling fingers she tore at the tangle. In the momentary silence she heard the shouted words: "Squirrelys . . . free. . . ." Someone *was* hunting, and Homer and Daniel had left their work to tell whoever it was that this land was now part of the Strawbridge Place. Freed from the snarl of hair and twigs, she moved forward quietly, not knowing what she would do—if—when. . . .

"This is Quaker land, no guns allowed." Daniel's strident voice came clearly to her ears.

"Since when, sonny boy? None a yur confounded Quaker fences here'bouts. Dis here's da Wider Pembroke's land, 'n I's bin a'huntin' dese woods since 'fore yah Quaker laddies be borned."

"Father paid gold for these ten acres a week ago Seventh Day," Homer said evenly. A string of curses fouled the woodland air.

Victory edged half her face around a big tree trunk. Homer and Daniel stood about fifteeen feet away, their backs to her, towering over three short men, each cradling a rifle with the practiced ease of hunters. One was Skinhead Poke; the other two were strangers.

Victory recoiled. Strangers with Skinhead! Skinhead was trouble enough alone. His small head was bald as a darning egg, and he kept it covered twenty-four hours a day with a once-green hunting cap, now black with filth. Rumor had it that he didn't even take it off when he slept. Victory thought of him as an evil Humpty Dumpty, for he was shaped like a small oval brown chicken egg.

"Paid gold—well now—ain't dat fancy-wancy. See?"

5

Skinhead hunched a shoulder at the two beside him. "Wurn't I a'tellin' yah dat ole man Strawbridge gots somethin' more dan jist 'taters 'n alfalfa 'n hosses on his place?" Suddenly his voice went ragged with hate. "Wurn't I a'tellin' yah 'bout dat deevil dawg chained up in dat dawghouse? Peace-lovin', God-fearin' Quaker folks doesn't needs no deevil dawgs, ifn yah asks me, less'en dey's gots somethin' ta hide. Ain't dat right?"

His two companions nodded. The three men looked up insolently, though Daniel stretched four inches over six feet, and Homer was only two inches shorter.

"Go hunt your squirrels on the other side of the railroad, Skinhead, and take your friends with you." Homer didn't raise his voice. "You know what happened the last time you trespassed on Strawbridge land."

"Trespassed!" Skinhead almost strangled on the word. "I wurn't trespassin' dat time yur deevil dawg done gots me, 'n I ain't a'trespassin' now. Yah's a'lyin' 'bout dis here land bein' sold ta yur Pa by da Wider."

"Strawbridges don't lie!" Daniel took a menacing step toward Skinhead, but Homer grabbed his arm.

"I'll do the talking, Daniel," he said.

"Tee-hee-hee," snickered Skinhead. "Dannul, yah minds yur ole brudder dere, dat's a good laddie. He'll git yah home safe ta dat purty mommy of yurn in one piece."

"Don't you dare even say my mother's name . . . !" Daniel lunged toward Skinhead, and Homer yanked him back, hard.

"Aw, gaw on home, sonny boys." Skinhead smiled, pleased to have roused Daniel's temper. "Tend ta yur 'taters 'n corn 'n dem grand hosses, while me 'n me hunter friends here does *man's* work 'n gits us'ns 'nough squirrelys fur a hot steamy stew." Skinhead's smile vanished, he shifted his rifle, then spit out one word:

"GIT!"

Rage poured through Victory. She bruised her forehead against the rough tree bark and willed—*do something, Homer!* Don't let Skinhead *bully* you like that. Let Daniel loose on him. . . .

"I says GIT, Quaker laddies," Skinhead repeated. Homer and Daniel didn't move.

"Aw let 'em be, Skinhead," one of his companions muttered. But Skinhead didn't want to hear him.

"I's a'goin' ta count ta THREE 'n ifn youse Quaker laddies ain't showin' yur heels by den, I got me two witnusses who'll swore I mistook youse fur a couple a gray squirrelys."

"Didn't know you could count that high," Daniel jeered, shaking off Homer's restraining hand. Skinhead's gun came up quickly, and he pointed it at Daniel.

"Yah no-count, stuck-up Quaker brat—" Skinhead swore the rest.

"Stow that gun before you do something you'll regret, Skinhead," Homer said. "What's gotten into you anyway? You really hunting—or out snooping again?"

"ONE!"

"We want no trouble like the last time, Skinhead," Homer said calmly, stepping toward his tormentor. "Plenty of squirrels in other woods around here." Forgetting Daniel, Skinhead moved his rifle and aimed it directly at Homer.

"TWO!"

"Look here, Skinhead." Homer advanced another step.

7

Skinhead's two companions stepped back and quickly shifted their rifles to their shoulders. Three slim gun barrels pointed at Homer. He stopped.

Victory's rage melted into fear. Her scream shattered the stillness as she flung herself from behind the tree. "Homer—Daniel—run!"

A rifle shot exploded.

Victory felt herself running as if in a dream; high floating steps that took so long—so long—to get anywhere. Before her, Homer twisted slowly to the ground. Daniel lunged to catch him, but missed. Skinhead turned and leaped across the clearing on short stubby legs. All three crashed into the underbrush, leaving a swath of broken branches and noise behind them.

"Homer!" Victory sobbed as she threw herself down beside him. "Homer—say something—Homer—please God—what—?"

Daniel, stunned by the shot and by Victory's sudden appearance, whirled toward the broken underbrush and shouted, "Skinhead, we'll get you for this," and started after the three. Victory's hands were racing over Homer's body. He groaned as her fingers came away, bloody and trembling, from his upper right thigh.

"Daniel, come back!" Victory screamed. "Get Beauty or Molly—hurry. There's blood. . . ." Daniel slowed, turned. He stood for an instant, dazed, then was beside her. Victory held up her bloody hands.

Daniel ran.

Victory tore at the buttons of her skirt and bundled it into a makeshift pillow for Homer. She wrapped her petticoat around his leg, but the blood wouldn't stop. With shaking fingers, she ripped off her blouse and pressed it against the wound as she'd seen Momma do, but still the red rivulet oozed through. Homer's cheeks twitched uncontrollably, but his eyes were open, and he looked up at her—asking?

"It's nothing, Homer. You'll be fine once we get you home to Momma. Just a nick." She talked too fast, avoiding his searching eyes. "Skinhead can't shoot, you know that," she rushed on. "Couldn't even shoot Blueboy that time he broke his chain and tore the kneecap right off Skinhead's breeches. Remember, Homer? You laughed the hardest when Blueboy came loping back to the barnyard and dropped that knee patch at Father's feet. Father thought Blueboy had scared Skinhead enough to keep him from snooping anymore, but. . . ."

Homer's blue eyes still stared up at her—asking?

"Don't you fret." Victory wondered how much longer she could keep up the pretense. "Momma'll fix you up right as rain like she always does when any of us get hurt or sick. . . ." A noise—breaking underbrush— thank the Lord! It was Daniel leading Molly.

The big horse stood quietly. "Grab Molly's bridle, Victory," Daniel said as he knelt, slipped his arms under Homer and lifted him with a great heave. Homer let out an agonized cry, but Daniel's strong arms clamped around him and held him so that he hung, stomach down, over Molly's back. "Lead away, Victory. On the double," Daniel commanded. Victory took the bridle and jerked the big horse forward.

"Mercy on us, what happened?" Momma came flying out the kitchen door onto the back porch. Faith, Victory's twin, was at her heels.

"Skinhead." Daniel didn't have to say more.

Momma's face blanched as she saw Homer's limp body hanging like a horseshoe across Molly's back, the drops of blood sending up little puffs of dust as they hit the bare ground of the barnyard.

"Victory," Momma said. "Run to the south apple orchard and get your father. Fly now."

As Victory headed for the orchard, she heard Momma call, "Peter, Paul!" As she raced through the horse pastures, she wondered what Daniel was saying about the shooting.

Father and several of his hired men were up on ladders trimming dead limbs from the blossoming trees. Victory waved to him, too breathless to call. He turned and saw her, leaped from the ladder and began to run toward her. "What's wrong, Victory? Where're your clothes?" He was already out of his shirt and had it about her shoulders.

"Homer—Skinhead shot him—and—"

Father didn't wait for more. He sprinted down the aisle between the trees, put his hand on the gatepost, and vaulted over the orchard-pasture gate in one giant leap. Too tired to keep up, she slipped her arms into the big shirt, climbed the gate, and there was Golden Dawn, her sides bulging with her first foal. Victory threw her arms about her little mare's neck and pressed her face into the yellow mane. Golden Dawn nickered and stood for a minute in Victory's choking grip, then broke away and trotted back to the other horses. Victory went on to the house. She was clammy with sweat and fear as she went into the kitchen and started up the narrow back stairs.

10

"We're not allowed up there," Faith warned, getting up from her knees where she was wiping up the floor. "Peter, Paul, Daniel, and Momma carried him up, and Father just came through here like a cyclone."

"How is—" Victory began, but Faith broke in.

"He was moaning something terrible. Momma wrapped her apron around his leg to keep the blood from dripping, but it didn't help any." Forgetting to clean up the trail of blood, she demanded, "What happened, Victory? Momma sent me in to stoke the range and get lots of water boiling, so I didn't hear what Daniel was saying. But you saw it, Victory. Tell me."

Victory collapsed into a chair and covered her face with her hands. "Momma can fix Homer, can't she, Victory?" Faith asked anxiously. "She always has before." She knelt before her sister. "Where're your clothes, Victory, and whose shirt is that?"

"Father's." Victory lifted her head and looked at her long cotton pantaloons. "Homer needed my clothes," she said in a raspy voice. "Oh, Faith, is he dead?"

"How should I know? I don't even know what happened, and if you don't tell me, I'll explode." In halting sentences Victory told Faith all she had seen and heard.

"So you screamed?"

Victory nodded yes.

"Think that's what made Skinhead shoot?"

"He'd counted TWO, Faith, and Homer and Daniel were just standing there and. . . ." Victory's fury surged up in her again as she remembered. "Would you have let Skinhead count THREE, Faith? Would you have?"

"Land sakes, Victory, I reckon you did right. But you know what Father's always said about Skinhead—that he's all bluff—and—"

"Then who shot Homer?" Victory said sharply.

"You saw it, I didn't," Faith said. "But I wish I had seen it," she said, eyes flashing. "It's the most excitement we've had around here since Constable Gilly and those two railroaders caught that last batch of runaways two weeks ago."

"You think I did right, screaming when I did?" Victory asked uncertainly. "Homer might not have gotten shot and—"

"You did right screaming," Faith said positively. "Homer and Daniel might *both* be shot if you hadn't done what you did." Then looking down at her twin she said, "Victory, go get some decent clothes on."

Victory nodded, got up, opened the dining room door and went toward the front hall and the winding front stairs.

Chapter 2

Victory crumpled onto the patchwork quilt on the double bed.

If she hadn't screamed . . . ?

The sounds of men's boots going down and then up the back stairs made her sit up. She jumped off the bed, threw off Father's shirt, jerked open the closet door, and took out a plain gray dress. Slipping a petticoat over her arms, she dressed. Then she went down the hall and pressed her ear to Homer's closed door. Hearing nothing, she opened it and started in.

Momma and Father, still shirtless, were leaning over Homer's body, which was half-covered with a blood-stained sheet. The teakettle and a pot of hot water steamed on the marble-topped washstand, and Father held a basin of brownish-red water from which Momma dipped and squeezed a red cloth. They were talking in low tones, but stopped abruptly as Victory appeared in the doorway. They didn't have to speak; such anxiety and fear filled their faces that Victory stumbled back out into the hall, pulling the door closed behind her.

Leaning against the wall, she felt guilt overwhelm

her. That scene was her fault! If Homer died, her scream
. . . she. . . . Taking the back stairs two at a time,
she found Paul, Peter, Daniel, and Faith all at the
table in the kitchen. "What are you doing just sitting
here?" Victory cried. "Why aren't you helping?"

"We did help," Peter said. "We took up boiling water,
the teakettle, and pitchers of cold water, and then
brought down that mound of bloody clothes there. Father said to stay here until he and Momma come down;
so now, there's nothing to do but wait."

"Wait." Victory looked at them with despair.

"Get hold of yourself, Victory," Daniel said. "Homer's
too tough for old Skinhead to do him in." Victory sat
down and watched the back door as the others were
doing—all except Paul who stared out the window to
the west, his manure-encrusted boots up on the big
scoured oval kitchen table; his fingers interlocked behind
his head.

A door opened and closed; footsteps sounded on the
back stairs. Paul's feet dropped silently to the floor, and
he swiped the flaked-off manure from the table with one
hand into the other. He looked about, desperate for a
place to put it, but there was no time, for Momma and
Father were already on the bottom step. With a twinge
of amusement, Victory watched Paul cram the manure
into his breeches' pocket.

"Hot enough in here to rile a saint," Father said as
he stepped heavily into the steamy kitchen behind
Momma. He wore a clean shirt. "To the parlor—quickly
—all of you." He pushed open the dining room door,
and Momma picked up her skirts and sailed through.
They all filed past Momma's prize glass china cupboard

14

and down the long front hall to the parlor's double doors. It was dark and cool inside, for Momma kept the shades drawn except when they had company. Father and Momma seated themselves on the horsehair couch, and the others scattered about the room—the boys sitting on the floor.

"We need a consensus," Father said softly. "In the past your mother has always patched us up when we got hurt, but this time it's different. The bullet's still in Homer's thigh, and probing for a bullet isn't woman's work—nor man's work either 'less he's got himself some doctor training—so that leaves us with that new Doctor Simmons. Right?"

"But we—you—we all suspect he's—" Peter began.

"No time for that now, Peter," Father said swiftly. "Your mother can't stop the bleeding, and someone's got to soon or. . . ."

Victory listened, benumbed.

"So the consensus vote is this: do we call Doctor Simmons or not?"

Everyone nodded yes.

"Thought so." Father jumped off the couch. "Daniel, Peter, saddle Gretchen Girl; and Daniel, you ride like Jehu to that doctor's fancy office. If he isn't there, go to Hoyle House. If he isn't either place, ask about, and if anyone knows where he is, go and fetch him here—*without fail*. But say nothing—*and I mean nothing*—about what's happened." Daniel rose and bolted out of the house, Peter beside him.

"But Father, the shipment?" Faith pointed over her shoulder in the direction of the long shed that stood on the opposite side of the large barnyard from the barn.

"You think I've forgotten them?" Father said so quietly that Victory hardly heard him. They heard Daniel come galloping around the house on Gretchen Girl and down the north side of the U drive. Peter, breathing hard, returned to the parlor and sank down on the floor again. Father pulled Momma to her feet and put an arm about her. "He'll find him," he said; then he asked her, "Is the shipment fed?" Momma nodded no against his shoulder.

"Victory, Faith, Peter, see to the shipment at once. Pack enough food and water for a couple of days. Peter and Victory, get down with the hampers and up again fast as you can. Faith, you busy yourself in the kitchen. I want everyone topside when that doctor comes. Paul, run and tell King what's happened and have him take over that crew in the apple orchard, then you get back to the smithy. I promised Abel Quimby his horses by tomorrow. Peter, be sure Blueboy is chained; then when you're finished down the Liberty Well, go fetch Beauty from the new north field. After all that, you can go on with exercising the horses. Twins, stay in the house. When that doctor fellow gets here, this must appear to be the most ordinary farm between Erie and Cleveland, except for Homer. Sarah, we'll stay with Homer."

Victory crowded up close to Peter, Paul, and Faith on the way back to the kitchen. Having work to do and people around might keep her growing guilt from destroying her.

Paul, a strange expression on his face, picked up some cold biscuits and began munching as he left the kitchen. Victory's stomach churned. "How can he eat . . . now?" she asked Peter as he stood on tiptoe to move

16

the pots of boiling water to the back of the range and then stoked the fire so the twins could warm food for the six runaways who were hiding in the cave down the Liberty Well.

"He's hungry." Peter laughed as he got the four hampers from their secret place behind the bins of flour in the pantry and placed them on the table. "We all know he's always hated the farm, except for the horses; and he hates even them since Father hauled him home last year after he lit out for the gold fields to join up with Joshua. Did you see that look on his face as he went out?" Victory nodded. "I've got a hunch he's been planning another escape for a long time, and now—with all this confusion about Homer—it might just be the right time to try again. And this time nobody's going to catch him—not even God. But forget Paul, Victory; tell me what happened in the woods."

Again Victory told her story, and with each word her guilt went deeper. Never before had she done anything that had resulted in such a terrible outcome. This morning she'd started for the new north field, carefree and looking forward to her thirteenth birthday; now in just hours she was something else. What, exactly, she didn't know. By the time she was finished, she could hardly talk, and tears rimmed her eyes.

"Let's change the subject," Faith said. "It's been ages since we got a letter from Joshua. Wonder if he's struck it rich yet?" She put some apples into one of the hampers.

"He won't show his face in Ashtabula until he does," Peter said as he went out to the pump to fill the water containers.

"The two of them—Joshua and Paul—all pride, self-ishness, wildness," Faith said. "Not Quaker-like one bit."

"But at least Joshua's written," Peter said, "so we know he's still alive."

"It'll be seven months next week since his last letter," Victory said, slicing dark bread for sandwiches that Faith then spread with butter and filled with thick slices of cold ham. Faith and Peter nodded, knowing that Victory kept track of things like that in her secret diary, locked up in a walnut box on the mantel in her bedroom. She wore the key on a string around her neck night and day.

"Ruben and Isaac are older than Joshua, and they *never* write, but Momma doesn't worry about them like she does Joshua."

"Well, they're safe," Peter said, latching the lids down on two of the filled hampers and putting them into a large flour sack. "Ruben's married, and Isaac's selling shoes in Cleveland."

The old wooden kitchen clock chimed two. Peter looked soulful, rubbed his stomach, and pointed to the shed. "Ready this minute," Faith said as she set the last hamper on the floor. "Have matches, Victory?"

Victory went to the matchbox by the range. Her mind was twisting and turning, and she felt dizzy as she and Peter stepped to the kitchen door. Redgirl, Faith's dog, sat in the shade of the back porch scratching and biting at her fleas. White, a mongrel watchdog, slept under the old apple tree by the outhouse. "It must be clear," Peter said, "or the dogs would be up, so let's go, Victory."

Peter carefully lifted the heavy sack to his shoulder as he walked out onto the porch, shuffled nonchalantly toward the shed, and entered the open doors of the section where the family carriage was kept. Victory went to the pump by the porch and filled the drinking dipper. She drank deeply of the winter-cold water, hoping it would settle her stomach and clear her mind, but as she hung the dipper back on its nail, she felt just the same. Slowly she followed Peter into the shed.

"You snail, Victory," Peter chided. "If we aren't topside before Spyglass Simmons gets here, we could complicate things. So, on your knees, girl, and I'll get the top one."

Chapter 3

Victory knelt; her fumbling fingers found the lower bolt, and she shot it back. Peter climbed up on the sawhorse in the corner and opened the top bolt. Together they pushed gently on the wall.

The end panel moved in. Peter jumped down and slipped through, easing the heavy sack before him, Victory close behind. He closed the moving section of the wall except for an inch or two to let in some light. Victory took a match from her pocket and lighted the candle in the candleholder.

They stood in a small room lined with wardrobes. Several trunks sat about on the floor, and an old rag rug was stretched beneath them. Peter pushed the secret panel closed, put the bag down, shoved one of the trunks against the panel, kicked back the edge of the rug, and seized the ring of iron. He gave the trapdoor a hard yank and leaned it against one of the trunks. Then he put one leg into the dark opening of the Liberty Well. Clinging to the iron steps mounted on the uneven stone sides, Peter took the bag and climbed down. Victory held the candle over the trapdoor to light his way. Once he reached the bottom, he set the bag down, and taking a match, he lighted the two candles in their holders on the dirt floor of the well.

"All clear, Victory," he called up. Quickly she blew out the secret room candle, picked up her skirts, eased herself through the trapdoor, and was beside Peter in an instant. He was already working on the locks and bolts on the thick wooden door in one wall of the well. The second double lock came open, and he pulled back on the ponderous door. The evil stale smell of the cave jumped out at them. Peter kicked two big stones against the door and tested it against them. The stones didn't move. There was no latch on the inside of that door, and if it swung closed, it would lock itself. Satisfied, Peter turned, swept up the bag, headed down the short stone corridor calling, "ERIE SHORES." The password echoed in the stinking darkness before him.

Victory lifted one of the candles from the floor and followed. At the end of the corridor, a huge natural cave loomed dark and silent. Not a candle glowed, not a sound stirred the blackness. "ERIE SHORES," Peter repeated as he placed the heavy bag on the bench by the table. The table was a clutter of dirty tin dishes, and thin lines of smoke stretched up from the three candles on the table. They had obviously been blown out moments before. "Don't be afraid, it's ERIE SHORES—with food. Come out now, quick, 'cause we can't stay. There's an emergency above."

Slowly three of the runaways emerged from the shadows. And the good smells from the hampers soon brought the other three from their hiding places.

"That 'mergency got to do wit us?" one of the slaves

21

asked. He was a small man with a scar that ran from his left ear down his neck to his shoulder.

"No, nothing to do with you. You're in the safest Underground Railroad station in all Ohio, so light those candles again and sit down and eat. There's enough food and water here for two days. You may not see any of us for a while, but don't get scared; we haven't forgotten you. You'll be off to Canada and real freedom sooner than you think."

"Freedom!" The small slave said the word like a prayer. The other five runaways just nodded.

"Got enough matches, candles?" Peter asked. Silence from the six blacks. Victory checked the boxes. Both were almost full.

"Yes. Enough for a week," she answered for them.

"Good. See you soon," Peter said, backing toward the corridor.

"Thank yah," said the small slave. He seemed to be the only one able to use his tongue today.

Victory picked up her candle, lighted the three smoking ones on the table, then turned and followed her brother. Yesterday she wouldn't have been able to leave the messy cave—the rumpled cots, the littered table, the candleholders buried in tallow, the filthy rug that filled the cleared level area on one side of the cave—but since Homer. . . . She ran past Peter, put the candle on the floor of the well, and began tugging at the heavy stones.

"Man's work," Peter said as he came striding after her on his short legs. Victory pulled herself up the iron steps as Peter locked the door. Victory moved the trunk holding the panel shut as Peter came up and closed the trapdoor. They slipped through the moving section of wall and bolted it shut behind them.

Victory's spirits lifted as she filled her lungs with fresh lake air. They edged past the carriage, squinting at the spring brightness before them. "I'm going to check Blueboy, then I'm coming in for a minute to see what's happened." They stepped from the shadow of the shed, and Victory hurried across the barnyard to the kitchen.

"The doctor here yet?" she whispered to Faith. Peter came in.

"Not yet," Faith said to both of them. She was rolling out pie dough. "Father came down for more boiling water, but he didn't say a word, and I didn't dare ask him about Homer." Victory sagged into a chair. If Faith didn't have the courage to ask Father about Homer, it must be terribly bad.

"I'm off," Peter said. "Wish I could stay to see Spyglass Simmons, but—"

"Don't call him that," Faith said. "Commodore Hoyle had that telescope and that spyglass in those two round towers 'cause he watched his ships through them, but has anyone ever seen Doctor Simmons looking through them?"

"But everyone says. . . ." Peter began.

"*Rumors!* All rumors, Peter Strawbridge," she called after him as he raced out, "and Quakers shouldn't listen to rumors." She looked at Victory. "Poor man," Faith went on. "Spyglass Simmons—new Doctor Simmons. He's been in Ashtabula two and a half years already, and still he's 'new.' I can see why there're rumors about him being in with Constable Gilly and Deputy Weed catching runaways 'cause you don't need a telescope and a spyglass for doctoring, but—"

"Oh, Faith," Victory broke in. "Why is Old Doc Patterson dead and not here to help when we need him. We could trust him for sure 'cause he was Father's best friend."

Faith frowned down at the dough. "It was Old Doc who brought Doctor Simmons here. And Old Doc loved Ashtabula and Lake Erie and all the people around here something fierce, so he wouldn't have brought anyone to take his place if he hadn't liked him, would he?"

"I reckon not," Victory muttered.

"As for new Doctor Simmons," Faith said. "He treated Louise for her croup this winter, and she missed only three First Days at her church and only four weeks of school the whole year. And with Old Doc she was out of school half the time—remember?"

"Louise Quimby," Victory scoffed, "plays sick just to get to stay home and be fussed over by that fussy fat mother of hers."

"Don't you dare say that about my very best friend, and you be respectful of your elders, Victory Strawbridge."

"Wonder what it's like to die?" Victory said almost inaudibly as she watched the rolling pin smooth and stretch the dough. She gnawed on her thumbnail. It seemed like a hundred hours since—since. . . . "God, bring the doctor soon, no matter what he is—spy, slave catcher, the devil himself. Bring him here right now!" she prayed.

It was as if God had been sitting in the next chair just waiting for her to ask, because just then all three dogs began to bark, and she heard faint hoofbeats. Faith dropped her rolling pin, cast her floury apron over a chair, and rushed into the dining room after Victory. When they reached the front door, Father was already there. A surging cloud of dust swirled up the north U drive.

"He's come," Father said quietly, as two horses emerged from the dust cloud. "Thank you, Lord." And he bounded over the six front steps in one spring and stood ready to catch the bridles of the slowing horses.

Chapter 4

Redgirl and White yapped and circled the lathered horses as they slowed and stopped. Daniel and the doctor slid from their saddles, and Father handed the reins of both horses to Paul, who had come running from the smithy. The doctor took his black bag from his saddlebag, then Paul led the spent horses away.

"Doctor Simmons, my father, Clayton Strawbridge," Daniel said, briefly but civilly, then left and followed Paul.

"Thank the Good Lord you're here, Doctor." The two men eyed each other as they shook hands. "My son, Homer, was shot two hours ago, and we can't stop the bleeding."

"Shot where—by whom?"

"In the right thigh," Father said, ignoring the second part of the question as he led the doctor across the porch and up the winding front stairs. Momma stood at the top, waiting. "My wife, Sarah."

"Good day, Doctor Simmons." Momma smiled warmly, then turning, she led the way into the sick room, leaving the door wide open.

Faith and Victory crept up the stairs and leaned against the banister that curved up the staircase and along the hallway. After a bit, since no one noticed them, they moved forward and leaned around the door-jamb.

Momma and Father hovered on one side of the spool bed, their backs to the door. Homer lay still as a corpse, but his eyes were open, watching the doctor. Victory couldn't look at his leg, for Homer . . . Homer—he'd taught her to ride and to train horses; he'd read poetry to her; he'd taught her to draw; he'd given her her diary; he'd. . . .

Doctor Simmons had stripped off his fashionable coat, rolled up his sleeves, and was washing quickly. Then he leaned over Homer and pressed his ear to his chest. Rising, he took in the room at a glance. "Get rid of that." He pointed to the basin of red water. "And bring up scalding water and cold as well. Then I'll need linens, pillows, blankets, and more hot water." Father took the basin, and as he came from the sick room, Victory reached for it saying:

"I'll get it." Father didn't smile.

"You and Faith get the linens and the rest." The twins did as they were told and put their loads on the trunk at the foot of Homer's bed. Father came in with the pot of steaming water and a clean basin and set them on the marble washstand. The doctor opened his black bag, and again he washed his hands hastily and dried them on the clean towel that Faith held out to him.

Victory tried not to look, but this time her eyes wouldn't obey her and fixed on the ragged swollen flesh of Homer's leg, still oozing blood. "Go away." The doctor waved the twins out of the room.

Momma glanced at them briefly, saying as they left, "Keep the water boiling." Faith took her hand, and Victory felt herself being led. She'd gone blind since seeing Homer's leg.

"You sit, Victory. I'll take care of things. You must feel awful about what you did," Faith said, obviously not realizing what her words said.

Victory crumpled into a chair and buried her head in her arms, blaming herself a hundred times for the scene upstairs. Faith stoked the range, went to the pump to fill two empty pots with water, and lifted them onto the stove top. Then she returned to her pies. Almost at once Momma's steps came on the stairs. "Faith, go get your brothers."

"What for?"

"Never you mind," Momma whispered. Faith left in a hurry.

"How is he?" Victory asked.

"Conscious," Momma said. "When Faith gets back, you two stay down here. Don't come upstairs for any reason—hear me?" Momma gave her a stern look, then went back to the sick room.

In just a few minutes, the pump handle rasped, and Daniel, Paul, and Peter came in and filed upstairs. Faith started to follow, but Victory shook her head. "Momma said we're not allowed."

"Then why can they go up?" Faith asked indignantly.

"I don't know," Victory said in a voice she didn't recognize as her own. Before she could utter another word, scream after scream tore through the house. Faith and Victory rushed together.

"Hold him tighter!" Doctor Simmons yelled. "Tighter
—tighter." Then the noises from the room upstairs
ceased as abruptly as they had begun. After several
minutes the twins drew apart. Their dresses were as wet
as if they had been swimming in the river.

There was the clatter of boots on the steps, and Father
strode to the range, opened the firebox door and peered
in. He seized the poker, swiped away the ashes clinging
to it, and thrust the iron into the fire. Victory's heart
turned over. Father's worry wrinkles, which appeared
only when there was the very worst trouble, were deep
gray grooves between his straight thick eyebrows. Yet,
with steady hands, he held the poker far into the roaring
firebox.

"Homer—will he be all right?" Faith ventured.

"The doctor probed while your brothers and I held
Homer down. He lost consciousness after those screams.
The bullet's out, thank God. How that doctor . . . it's
a miracle, that's all." He pulled the poker from the firebox. It glowed pink, and he pushed it back into the
flames.

Victory stood, mesmerized. The poker was to sterilize
the wound. Her heart raced in time with the ticking of the clock. Father withdrew the poker, now red-
hot, and rushed across the kitchen.

Victory sank to the floor. Faith hurried to her, pulled
her head against her shoulder. They waited tensely for
more screams, but none came. Then the stench of burning flesh drifted into the kitchen.

Victory vomited.

"Stop that, Victory," Faith said, pushing Victory into
a chair. More vomit poured out onto the table. "Think

what Homer's going through," Faith chided her sharply. "And he didn't even yell this time." The kitched smelled vile. "Go wash yourself while I clean up in here," Faith said, pushing her twin out the door toward the pump.

Their brothers came down, faces grim, and headed back to their chores. Faith came out to the pump. Victory suddenly straightened her shoulders and began to wash. "Did the boys say anything about. . . ?"

"No," Faith said and returned to the kitchen. Victory finished cleaning her dress, and after a quick look up at Homer's window, she went inside, her feelings more under control. Just then the sick room door creaked open, there were footsteps, then voices.

"It'll be forty-eight hours at least before we know if he's going to keep that leg."

"It's up to you and the Good Lord," Father said.

"The Good Lord?" the doctor questioned. "More depends on the stamina of the patient, the care he gets, old-fashioned grit, luck. Nothing more I can do now, but I'll be here early in the morning. Sarah, give him this powder mixed with water when he gets restless. Force it down him if you have to." As the three went down the front stairs, Victory and Faith crept through the house to the front hall.

"Doctor Simmons, I'd like your promise that you'll say nothing about this accident to anyone," Father said.

"I shall say nothing," the doctor replied simply. Victory leaned around the coat and hatrack—behind which she and Faith were hiding—and saw the two men seal their promise with a handshake. Then Father went out onto the porch and let out a halloo for Daniel to bring the doctor's horse. When Daniel came, Doctor Simmons

30

slipped his black bag into his saddlebag, mounted, tipped his hat to Momma and said, "Good day, Sarah and Clayton. Until tomorrow." He kicked his horse and was gone.

Momma swayed toward Father. "Oh, Clayton, Homer *has* to be all right."

"He will be." Father caught her and held her close. Victory left the coatrack and went into the cool dark parlor, where she threw herself on her knees before the horsehair couch.

"Oh, Lord, Lord—take my leg, not Homer's." She looked up at the framed motto over the couch.

Do not slight them, to wit, the Ethiopians, the blacks now, neither any man or woman upon the face of the earth; in that Christ died for all, both Turks, Barbarians, Tartarians, and Ethiopians; he died for the tawnies and for the blacks, as well as for you that are called white . . . Christ, I say, shed his blood for them as well as for you . . . and hath enlightened them as well as he hath enlightened you. . . .

GEORGE FOX

Those words were the foundation of Father's Underground Railroad station, and Momma had made a sampler of them. But the message written by the founder of the Quaker faith couldn't calm her terror or still her guilt, and she slipped to the floor into oblivion.

Chapter 5

Victory felt Father lift her gently in his arms, carry her to the kitchen, and place her in a chair at the table. Momma pressed a wet towel to her forehead. Everyone sat in his regular place except Homer.

"Victory?" Father said. "Do you think it was Skinhead who shot Homer?"

"He was counting. . . ."

"But did you see smoke coming from his gun after the shot?"

Smoke? "I don't remember smoke," she answered, forcing herself to sit straight in her chair. Then she asked quickly, "Father, if I hadn't screamed, do you think Skinhead would have shot Homer?" But Father was intent on who had held the smoking gun.

"Daniel, do you?" Daniel gave him a wild, quarrelsome look.

"No, I don't remember smoke," he said in a loud positive voice, "but it was Skinhead all right and—"

"Two eyewitnesses and no proof," Father interrupted.

"But—" Daniel's face reddened, and his thick dark eyebrows, replicas of Father's, drew together in a savage line. "I know I—"

"No smoke," Father said, spreading his hands in a gesture of futility.

"There was a third eyewitness," Victory said.

Father gave her a glance of approval, but said, "That one's unconscious."

"So Skinhead gets clean away again?" Daniel said. The question was a challenge. Father merely glanced at him.

"Bad business, this," he said, half to himself. Then, turning toward them all, he said, "Always thought Skinhead was bluff—no real stuffing in him that would make him shoot a man."

"But you were wrong," Daniel said, satisfaction in his voice. Still Father paid him no mind, but the two worry-wrinkle grooves cut deeply into his tanned nose bridge. In the steamy kitchen the only sound was of the ticking of the old wooden clock. Suddenly it chimed four times.

"What?" Father squinted at the clock. "Can it be *that late?*" He got up. "Nothing more we men can do for Homer now, and the Quimby horses are waiting, and King's still down yonder in the. . . ."

But no one moved as Daniel said, "You mean you aren't going after Skinhead—now?"

"No."

"You're going to let him get away with half-killing Homer, same as he got away with trespassing last month and poaching last fall and all the—"

"Enough!" Father cut Daniel off. "Honor thy father and thy mother. . . ." He didn't finish and pointed toward the smithy. "Move." He followed his three sons out the door. Momma went up silently to be with Homer. The twins, abandoned in the kitchen, looked at each other.

"Faith—my scream? Have I killed Homer?"

"Victory, won't do a bit of good worrying about that 'cause nobody knows, and like Father said, there's nothing we can do. What's done is done and can't be undone," she said in a practical Momma-voice. "Except for catching Skinhead."

"Wonder why Father didn't take a consensus vote on chasing Skinhead?" Victory asked.

"There're lots of things Father decides without votes. Votes—consensuses . . ." Faith sighed. "Victory, you know what I pray every night? That Father'll give up the secret and be an ordinary farmer, and then Louise can come spend the night and—"

"Louise Quimby's a gossip, so it's better she doesn't come stay—"

"Don't you dare say that about my best friend," flared Faith. "Louise has had me to her house so many different times that I'm beholden to her for ever and ever. Father invites people here anytime he wants, to avoid suspicion, but I can't—"

"But you know why." Victory heard her voice coming out evenly. "He gets more cautious all the time, especially since that Second Fugitive Slave Law got passed by Congress."

"But that was two whole years ago," Faith cried. "Father's quoted that Section Seven to us so often I know it by heart." She giggled, then jumped up on a chair, spread her legs, pulled at an imaginary beard, and tried to wrinkle her smooth little nose into worry wrinkles.

In manly tones she began, "Second Fugitive Act, 1850, Sept. 18." Father's voice seemed to be coming from her mouth.

". . . or shall *harbor* or *conceal* such fugitive, so as to prevent the discovery and arrest of such person as a fugitive . . . be subject to a fine of not exceeding *one thousand dollars,* and *imprisonment not exceeding six months,* . . . and shall moreover *forfeit and pay,* by way of civil damages, . . . the sum of *one thousand dollars for each fugitive* so lost. . . ."

Victory felt so glum she hardly listened to Faith at first, but her twin's ridiculous impersonation made her smile in spite of herself. By the end of her quoting, Faith had become so agitated that she leaped down from her chair, stomped her foot and cried, "I fairly *hate* our station! If it weren't for King and Clarasue and Lilac and Luke, I'll bet we wouldn't have it. Just because they're Negro and work for Father. . . ."

Victory put her finger to her lips and looked toward the back stairs. Faith clapped her hand over her mouth. "I didn't mean to holler like that, Victory, honest I didn't," she whispered. "But runaway slaves. Who cares about them anyway! Hayrides and taffy pulls, that's what I want on Seventh Day nights instead of Liberty Wells and Bible barrels and toting food to runaways. Louise says—"

"If you've given even the slightest hint to Louise Quimby about Father and King running a station on the Underground Railroad, you've—you've—" Victory stopped, so horrified at her twin's folly that she forgot Homer.

"She won't tell." Faith tossed her head. " 'Cause. . . ."

" 'Cause why?"

" 'Cause I've got enough sense to keep the Strawbridge Secret safe. I don't fancy going to *jail* one little bit." Momma's step came on the stairs. Victory was beside her the instant she came into the kitchen.

"How is he?"

"The same."

"Momma, if I hadn't screamed . . . ?" Victory began. Momma pulled her close.

"Victory, stop vexing yourself. We'll never know what your scream had to do with it, but it doesn't matter anyway. What happened wasn't your fault. Hear me—*wasn't your fault.*" Victory looked deep into Momma's eyes. Momma's arms were about her, and Victory felt herself hugged as never before, and with that her guilt and terror were eased.

Finally Momma released her, saying, "Your father may think Skinhead's harmless, but I've always thought he's contrary enough to shoot a person just for fun. Clayton's going to have to settle with him once and for all, after this. Poaching and snooping and bullying and telling lies about us are one thing, but using Strawbridges for target practice is quite another." She looked out the kitchen door. "Such a beautiful spring day, and this has to happen. Sometimes I wish. . . ."

". . . that Father were just an ordinary farmer, and that there weren't any you-know-what?" Faith finished for her. Momma turned away from the doorway, a strained look on her pretty face.

36

"That's what you and Daniel and Paul wish, isn't it?"

"Yes," Faith said boldly. "Momma, when can Louise come sleep overnight?"

"Faith, shame on you. How can you ask about a trivial thing like that when your brother's lying upstairs, a shipment below, Golden Dawn about to foal, and no spring cleaning begun." She sounded so discouraged that Victory wanted to run to her and try to cheer her up, but Momma did it herself. She squared her rounded shoulders and asked, "Who made the pies?"

"I did," Faith said.

"Those'll taste mighty good tonight." Momma smiled at Faith. "You girls will have to tend to supper—I can't leave Homer. When I'm away from him, I'm afraid." Momma went up the stairs, holding her skirts high before her.

"I'm afraid," echoed in Victory's ears and reechoed in her heart.

Chapter 6

Faith was asleep. If she were condemned to the gallows at sunrise, Faith would sleep her last night away without waking. But not Victory. She lay on her stomach on the floor in the corner of their square bedroom, the candle in its pewter holder casting a small circle of light over her diary.

May 13, 1852, Fifth Day
   Momma said that it wasn't my fault, and that I'm not to blame for what happened today, but. . . . She meant it, and I felt better for a little while, but now—it's wrong again. I feel awful. You see, Homer almost got killed today by Humpty Dumpty S. I screamed. That scream— it's haunting me. I don't know what to do about it. I can't talk to Homer as I usually do. . . .

"Victory?" Momma's plain white nightgown moved into the circle of light. "Put that diary away and get into bed."

"I was in bed, but I couldn't sleep, so I started this."

Momma nodded understandingly.

"Come sit with me then. That powder the doctor left isn't doing a thing for Homer, and you could help me with a couple of things." Victory quickly locked her diary away, blew out her candle, and went to Homer's room. She stopped at the bed's footboard. Spots of blood stained the white counterpane, and Homer's head turned back and forth, back and forth, on an unnaturally arched neck.

"What can I do, Momma?" she asked.

"I need some fresh cold water." Victory picked up the empty pitcher. A half-moon lighted her way to the pump. Blueboy growled and came out of his doghouse, but she quieted him with a word. She filled the pitcher and returned, bolting the kitchen door behind her.

"Good," Momma said as she came softly into the room. She took the cold water, wrung out a rag, and placed it on Homer's forehead. "There, that should make him feel better." But Homer, his hair a tangle of thin dank strands, continued his tormented head-rolling. "Doctor Simmons said that powder would ease him," Momma said anxiously. She kept exchanging the cold rags. Then she said, "I've been so worried about Homer that I haven't even thought about the shipment."

"Peter and I took enough food down for two days before the doctor came."

"If that doctor only knew how close he'd been. . . ." Momma broke off. "But I mustn't slander him. It's only a rumor that he's a spy for Constable Gilly."

"You think Skinhead knows about this shipment?" Victory asked.

"Wish I knew what Skinhead knows," Momma said.

"Since that railroad gang came, he's toadied up to them, introduced them to the local gaggle of slave catchers. He snoops everywhere, but he's been snooping around here more and more lately, and it isn't just squirrels he's after." She put a fresh cloth on Homer's head. "When Skinhead was a young'un I used to pity him."

"Pity him?" Victory asked in great surprise.

"Yes, pity him," Momma repeated. "His momma dying and. . . ."

"When was that?" Victory asked.

"Years and years ago. Nice woman, church-going—how she ever got mixed up with Polecat Poke I'll never know. The week she died, he left town for good."

"How old was Skinhead then?"

"About five, I reckon."

"But who took care of him?"

"Ned Nardico."

"Who's he?"

"Owned the Lighthouse Saloon. Ned let Skinhead sleep under the stairs there, kept him alive when no one else cared. But Ned's long dead now, and Skinhead's grown up."

"Momma, what's Skinhead's real name?"

"Samuel."

"Who started calling him Skinhead?"

"Don't know—just always was. The Good Lord forgive me for speaking ill of anyone, but Skinhead and his lowdown rowdies are a plague on this town." She exchanged the rag on Homer's forehead. "But he's never harmed anyone that I've heard tell of—until today."

"Why doesn't the town tar and feather him and ride him out of here on a rail . . . ?" Victory began.

Momma hushed her.

"Don't wish that on anyone, Victory, not even Skinhead. I saw a man tarred and feathered once, and I'll never forget that night as long as I live."

Victory understood at once. She would never forget *this day*. "Was it worse than Homer's leg?"

"It was different," Momma said. "Those long knives —gleaming in the light of the fire under the pot of burning tar—those are what I'll never forget. There was a mob of townspeople—even children, for I was there—ranting and rushing about, the smell of the boiling tar, then those knives, stabbing feather ticks and pillows; and feathers everywhere, the tar brushes, the shouts—" She broke off. "Oh, Victory, how I love my twins." Momma's arms reached out and caught her up and hugged her close. "I can talk to you two as if you both were grown up instead of just little girls."

"We're not little girls any more," Victory said, her face pressed hard against Momma's nightgown. "We're almost thirteen."

Momma's arms loosened. "I'm going to have to think about your birthday party very soon."

Downstairs the clock chimed twice. "Two o'clock," Momma said. She wrung out a cloth as if she wished it were Skinhead's neck. "Into bed with you. I shouldn't have let you stay up so late. Now scoot."

"Momma, just once more. My scream. . . ."

"I thought we'd settled that, Victory. You did what you believed to be right, and that's all any of us can ever do in a crisis like that. If you hadn't screamed, Homer might have been shot in the heart, and we'd be planning a funeral, not keeping a bedside vigil."

41

Momma leaned down and kissed the end of Victory's nose. "Now I don't want to hear another word about that scream. I wish I could make you stop fussing about it, but you'll just have to do that for yourself. Now off to bed with you."

Victory went down the darkened hallway to her room. ". . . you'll just have to do that for yourself."

It was a long time before she slept.

Chapter 7

The cocks were crowing as if they had discovered dawn
for the very first time when Faith poked Victory awake.
"Wonder if Father's going after Skinhead today?" she
said as she stretched and reached for the candle. Victory
lay with open eyes, but all she wanted to do was go back
to sleep. Asleep, she didn't feel that tightening inside
her that a sermon from Momma couldn't help.

Faith splashed water from the pitcher into the wash-
bowl. "Cold," she panted, squeezing out the wet washcloth. "I'm going to wash at the pump."

The clammy washcloth hit Victory in the face. "Lazy-
bones," Faith said. Sitting up, Victory threw the cloth
back at her twin. "At least you're awake," Faith said as
she ran out. In two minutes she was back. "Get up, Victory, the doctor's coming." She began to dress quickly
but carefully. "Isn't he the handsomest, nicest man
you've ever seen, Victory? I took a shine to him the
minute I saw him, in spite of all—"

"You can't like him." Victory threw off the quilt.
"He may be dangerous."

"That makes him all the more exciting." Faith

43

grinned, and with a flounce of skirts went out, kicking the door closed behind her.

Victory washed and dressed, set the room to rights, snuffed out the candle, and went down the hall to Homer's room. Peter sat in the chair changing the rags on Homer's face. "How is he?" she whispered.

"Bad." Peter's lips formed the word but no sound came.

Coming into the kitchen, bright with lantern light, she saw Momma's back bending over the range. "Homer?" Victory ran to her.

"Worse," Momma said without turning, "but the doctor's coming within the hour so. . . ."

"Where's Faith?"

"Asked me about Homer, then before I could turn about, she ran out with Redgirl. You want to take a quick look at Golden Dawn?"

Victory ran out the kitchen door and raced across the shadowy barnyard. The stable doors were wide open, and she went to the paddock outside Golden Dawn's stall. Paul and Father were there, Father holding a lantern high. Golden Dawn stood in the far corner kicking at her bloated sides. "She's about due," Father said as Victory came up quietly and stood beside him. "Hey, daughter, your little mare is going to be a mother before the hour's out or I'm a blind old horse thief."

"I'll bet you a gold dollar it'll be two hours," Paul said.

"Hummmmm." Father regarded him soberly, knowing he knew horses almost as well as Peter. "Gambling isn't one of the ways of the Lord, but as long as your mother doesn't hear about it, Paul, I'll take you up on that." Paul merely nodded and walked to the barn to help Daniel with the chores there.

"Scat, Victory. Your mother needs help. She was up all night with Homer." Victory raced to the pump, where she found Faith and Redgirl. It was then that Victory noticed Faith was wearing her second-best dress, the one with the white crocheted collar. They washed and burst into the kitchen that smelled of baking apple pies and perking coffee. Redgirl followed, but at Faith's command, she turned and stood just behind the doorsill.

"Father says this hour, and Paul says in two hours," Victory declared.

"Wish Redgirl was that close to having her puppies," Faith said.

"A foal on top of everything else." Momma's eyes were ringed with dark circles, and she was still in her nightgown with an apron over it. She poked at the six balls of bread dough rising on the back of the range. "This is going to be an extra special day for you, Victory. Now you girls keep an eye on my pies and get breakfast. Make some extra as well, for the doctor might be staying and make plenty of strong coffee." Momma picked up a mug from the shelf above the range and took a swallow. "And put some pots of water on to heat. I'd better go make myself decent before the doctor comes." One hand went to her untidy braid and with the other she carried her coffee mug as she hurried up the back stairs.

The twins got the pots of water and teakettle heating. Faith couldn't stop smiling at the thought of the doctor being right there in their kitchen, eating breakfast that she'd prepared, talking to Father and Momma while she watched him. She yanked open the oven and looked at the four pies. Steam and juices issued through the crescent-shaped slits in the top crusts, and the fluted rims were amber brown. "Victory, run to the springhouse and bring that special yellow cream. We'll have it this morning on the pies—if the doctor stays," she said. "I'm almost glad Homer got shot because we've finally met Doctor. . . ."

Victory fled. *That doctor*—pies—special yellow cream —the thought made her dizzy. What was real? Golden Dawn's foal was real, Father's and Paul's bet was real, Homer's leg was real. Yesterday—just yesterday— nothing had troubled her more than wanting a perfect birth for Golden Dawn, but today. . . .

She returned just as the men came from the barn. They washed hastily in the icy pump water, and then hurried into the warm kitchen. Momma came down just as they entered. She looked like blueberries and cream in her midnight blue gingham, with the white shawl that she had crocheted about her shoulders. Father's eyebrows arched in surprise, but he said nothing as everyone sat down. "Victory, tend to breakfast. You seem to be the only one dressed for work today," he added, looking hard at Faith.

Victory ladled out buckwheat batter onto the round, greased, griddle. Everyone bowed his head in silent prayer, even Victory.

Scorched!

The smell ended the silent praying, and the pancakes came up burned black. Sheepishly, Victory scraped them off the griddle and poured out fresh rounds of batter. Plates and bowls of food—soda biscuits, gravy, sausages, butter, homemade strawberry jam, maple syrup, fried potatoes with onions, cooked oatmeal, baked apples, and several other things—passed about the table. Victory hovered over the second batch of pancakes, and they were perfect. She put them on a tin platter and placed them before Father's plate. He took five and passed the platter to Daniel. As he did so, Daniel asked, "Are we going after Skinhead today?"

"Yes," Father said, "but Homer's first, the Quimby horses're second, Golden Dawn's third—"

"You mean he's fourth?" Daniel demanded. "Then let me go after him—alone—now."

"No," Father said. Daniel bristled, then shrugged away his disappointment.

"Reckon it doesn't matter anyway," he said. " 'Cause it's too late. He'll be gone by now—pulling one of his disappearing acts."

"Daniel," Father said, "you're to come to town with me after the doctor's gone this morning when we deliver the Quimby horses."

"But what about Golden Dawn . . . ?" Victory began, but stopped as the front door knocker resounded through the house. Everyone leaped up, and Momma was already halfway through the dining room when Father's firm quiet voice stopped everyone in his tracks.

"Daniel, come with us to tend his horse, then come back and finish your breakfast. You're to take charge of the hired hands. I want planting done in the southwest cornfield and the Widow Pembroke's lot cleared. Get them started soon as you can, 'cause you're coming

47

to town with me. The rest of you finish eating. Paul, check on Golden Dawn, then get the Quimby horses ready. It's been just half an hour. . . ." Victory heard him almost give himself away about the bet. "Peter will help you as soon as he's had his breakfast. And remember—the name of Skinhead Poke isn't to be mentioned under any circumstances." Then he and Daniel caught up with Momma in the long hall.

The twins and Paul crept into the dining room. The bolt on the big front door slammed back and Father said heartily, " 'Farm early' you've come, Doctor Simmons. Daniel'll see to your horse."

Footsteps on the wide front stairs. The three listeners retreated to the kitchen to wait for Peter. When he came down, Victory waved the pancake turner at him. "What's happening?"

"Don't know," Peter said as he began his breakfast. "They shooed me out and closed the door."

"Oh dear." Victory turned back to the range to hide her face from the others. That tightness inside her made her all jittery, and she burned another batch of pancakes. But when Daniel returned from the stable, Victory turned and asked, "Golden Dawn?"

"Coming along," was all he said. Victory looked at the clock. Father would lose his bet in just fifteen more minutes.

Chapter 8

Father came down for hot water, but no one dared ask him what was going on upstairs. The boys finished breakfast with Momma's pies swimming in the special yellow cream. Daniel threw his napkin onto the table and complained, "Why won't Father let me go after Skinhead? I can't wait to get my hands on that little louse, and—Father or no Father—I'll. . . ." He didn't finish and slammed out of the kitchen to see to the hired crew.

". . . kill him," Paul finished.

"La de da—such sweet Quaker talk." Peter ran out the door before Paul could catch him. The twins cleared the table, then set new places. It wasn't long before Father came down to get a second steaming pot.

"Homer?" Victory couldn't hold the question in.

"The doctor's given him some new . . ." Father hesitated, a grin at the corners of his mouth. ". . . medicine that he guarantees will relax Homer, put him to sleep, and build up his blood as well."

"Is he staying for breakfast?" Faith asked, trying to keep her voice casual, but failing.

"I hope not." Father lowered his voice. "He's one man I don't want to see any more of the farm than I can help. But just in case—is everything ready?" he asked over his shoulder as he headed for the stairs.

"Yes," the twins said together.

It was only a few minutes before Momma preceded the doctor and Father into the kitchen. Faith fluttered up to him. "You can put your bag right here, Doctor Simmons," she said, smiling up at him.

"Thank you." He smiled back. Then he turned toward Momma, pulled out a chair from the table and, with easy grace, seated her. Victory saw his face, and she knew at once that he was as tired as Momma. Had he been up all night doctoring some other patient? Before Father could call for coffee, Victory gathered up her apron, picked up the hot handle of the pot, poured a blue and white cup full. But before she could set it on the table, Faith took it from her and put it down before the doctor. He pushed it over to Momma and said, "Here, Sarah. This'll put some life into you."

Victory saw Momma purse her lips, and she accepted the cup with a curt, "Thank you." Hurriedly Victory poured two more cups, and Faith set them before the doctor and Father. Father poured almost half the sugar bowl into his and stirred mightily.

"Bring it on, daughters. I'm hungry as a bear," Father said, perhaps trying to make up for Momma's coldness. As the twins served them, the doctor called them by their correct names. "Most people have trouble telling them apart at first, Doctor, but you've gotten them straight right off," Father said.

"Faith's eyes are brown—the color of my eyes—and

Homer and Victory both have blue eyes," the doctor answered around a large bite of pancakes.

"Oh ho," Father blurted out. "Observant of you, Doctor, most observant indeed."

Momma ate nothing, just sat holding her coffee cup and drinking quickly. As soon as she finished she got up, refilled her cup, and without a parting word to Doctor Simmons, started up the stairs. Before she could close the door, the doctor was on his feet and calling after her. "Get some sleep, Sarah, or I'll be tending you next." The door closed firmly in his face.

Victory felt stranger than ever. Why was Momma being so rude? She poured more batter on the griddle, but just then boots drummed across the barnyard, and Peter burst through the door.

"Golden Dawn, she's. . . ." Chairs scraped, and the kitchen emptied. Victory glanced at the clock. Father owed Paul a gold dollar. But that didn't matter now. Only Golden Dawn did. She raced out of the door.

As she entered the stables, Victory looked down to see the pancake turner still in her hand. Wheeling, she raced back to the house. Too excited to think, she seized the griddle, smoking with scorching batter, by its hot handle. A choked cry filled the kitchen as she dropped the griddle from her burned hand. Batter slithered everywhere. Her hand was on fire, but all she could think of was Golden Dawn, so leaving the mess on the floor, she raced back out. By the time she reached the stables, everyone was standing by the paddock outside Golden Dawn's stall. The mare was pawing at the grass and snorting. Then she lay down, only to get up again and move restlessly about the paddock. The birth hadn't begun yet, and the men were talking.

"Four sons and two daughters—a fine family for sure—but, Clayton, the Strawbridge Place is huge, so you must need—"

"King and his family work for me, and—" Father began, but the doctor interrupted.

"You mean that colored family I've seen in town now and then?"

"Yes." Father said. "And I've other hired help as well."

"Free coloreds," mused the doctor. "To me, coloreds are slaves."

"I have three other sons, but they're grown and have left home," Father explained, then asked Peter, "How long has Golden Dawn been snorting and pawing?"

"About fifteen minutes," Peter said. Victory knelt as close to Golden Dawn as she could and crooned to her. The mare's ears twitched in recognition, but she didn't come to Victory. Instead she lay down in the far corner of the paddock and didn't get up again.

"She hears you." The doctor went down on one knee beside Victory. "But she knows that the birthing's begun."

"Everything has to go right for her—not like Homer," Victory said passionately.

"Homer's doing just fine," Doctor Simmons assured her.

"Oh, I didn't mean that the way it sounded." Victory looked up, apologizing. "You've done a wonderful job with Homer, and we're all so obliged. . . ."

"Yes," Faith said, kneeling on the other side of the doctor. "Without you, Homer would be dead." Quickly the doctor changed the subject.

"You love horses, don't you, Victory?"

"I raised Golden Dawn," Victory said. "Homer helped me, but I trained her and have ridden her everywhere."

"Where is everywhere?"

"Around the farm and. . . ." Victory faltered. Something told her that she was being more than casually questioned. She glanced at him out of the corner of her eye. How could he be so wicked—a slave catcher—when he was so handsome? No wonder Faith was smitten. His blond beard was close-clipped, running down from his sideburns in a narrow brush along his chin with a graceful arch circling up beneath his large straight nose. His skin was smooth beige, his eyes deep brown—as he'd said—just like Faith's.

"Do you twins like living on a farm?" he asked. Then before either could answer, he said, "You see, I grew up in Baltimore, so country living is something I don't know much about except what I've learned in my time here in Ashtabula. I didn't like the city, and that's why, when Doctor Patterson invited me to join his practice, I came west. I suppose you both know that the Strawbridge Place is a legend among the people hereabouts. They say that since this new house and barn and all those other buildings went up three years ago, it's the showplace of this corner of Ohio. Do you feel their envy?" He looked from one to the other, his face friendly and open.

Victory turned away to look at Golden Dawn. Just then a convulsion went through the little mare and water came spilling from her. Then a bulging membrane-like sack appeared in her dilated opening. The

53

doctor pointed. "You can see the foal's feet now." They all waited quietly and within minutes the foal, wrapped in a clear sack that looked like spun sugar, began to emerge, front feet first, its tiny head lying across them. It came from Golden Dawn in a diving position, and finally lay free on the grass, the ruptured umbilical cord trailing on the ground.

Victory sat glued to the fence, her burned hand forgotten. Golden Dawn got up at once, turned, and began to lick her foal all over. Then she began nudging her baby until the foal was forced to its knees, then finally wobbled to its feet. Now Golden Dawn circled it, nuzzled it, pushed it, trying to get it to begin nursing. The foal fell down, but she forced it to its feet again, and this time she succeeded in getting it to nurse.

"A perfect birth," said Father quietly. "Peter, keep an eye on her, but I think she'll be able to manage from here on by herself. To work; the morning's half done," he said even though the sun was still low in the eastern sky. "Daniel, the doctor's horse."

The group went around and into the stable. Victory lagged behind, watching Golden Dawn and the nursing foal, wanting to stay with them—to be alone. Then she remembered Momma's curious rudeness to the doctor, so she hurried to catch up with the others, and stumbled and fell. She threw out her hands to break her fall, and the brittle straw punctured the blisters on her burned left palm. Her scream filled the stable. The doctor whirled and rushed back to her. "What's wrong, Victory?" Victory turned up her left hand.

The others gathered around, and Daniel demanded, "How'd you do that?"

"Never mind," the doctor spoke quickly. "Clayton,

can you carry her to the house or should I get my bag?"

"I'll carry her," Father said, and he lifted Victory into his arms. She buried her face in his rough shirt and tried to stifle her crying, for she felt ashamed to give in to her pain after watching the birth struggle that Golden Dawn had just endured without a whimper.

Faith pranced beside the doctor. "How do you like country living, Doctor Simmons?" she asked.

"Very much."

"Would you like to live on a farm like this?"

"Yes. This is such a large and beautiful and well-organized operation, it would be a pleasure to be part of it. I never realized before just how close to the Grand River you are. How far down does your father's property go?"

"Down to the second covered bridge and—"

"Run ahead and get the kitchen door." Father interrupted, before she could reveal more.

Once in the kitchen Father settled Victory in a chair, and the doctor opened his black bag. He washed his hands at the pump, then took Victory's injured palm and looked at it. "Should be more careful with hot griddle handles," he said, smiling. Victory barely nodded. The discarded griddle—the burns—again the accurate observations of the doctor shook her. What else had he seen—recorded—filed away in his memory? Close to Grand River—shipping slaves by boat to Canada—it fits like a glove, doesn't it, Doctor? she thought as she watched him take some things from his bag.

The back stairs door opened, and Momma came sweeping into the kitchen. "What's all this commotion?" she asked sharply.

"Victory burned her hand, then fell on it in the

straw," the doctor said.

"Pshaw," Momma said, looking from Victory's hand to the doctor's open bag. "Doctor Simmons," she said pointedly, "bullets are one thing, but burned hands, cuts, fevers—I've kept us all patched up and alive till now, and I intend to go right on doing so."

"Very well." The doctor closed his bag. "Then with your permission, I'll take one last look at Homer and be on my way." He and Father went up the stairs, and Faith followed, eager to be close to the doctor as long as she could.

Victory was so relieved to have Momma tend her that she smiled in spite of the pain. "That's my brave girl," Momma said, but her voice was still hard. Then, trying to regain her usual gentle manner, she asked, "And the foal?"

"Oh, Momma, if only you could have been there." Victory forgot her hand and Momma's strange behavior. "It's the most beautiful foal in the world."

"Glad something's doing well around here," Momma muttered as she left to get the medicine chest in the parlor. The clock chimed eight. Father, Faith, and the doctor came down the back stairs.

"My regards to Sarah, Clayton, and I'll be here 'farm early' tomorrow. And Clayton, see that she goes to bed —she needs sleep." Father whistled, and Peter came with the doctor's horse. Faith stood on the porch as the doctor mounted, and she waved and waved after him as he rode down the lane.

Victory didn't utter a sound as Momma fixed her hand. It hurt—hurt so! Homer, Golden Dawn—by rights it was her turn now.

Father came stamping in. "Glad he's off the place," he said. Then shaking his head he went on. "A gentleman—to the manner born—as the saying goes. So what's he doing way out here in this pipsqueak country town? Eyes like an eagle's, and I'll wager a memory like an elephant's. But no time to puzzle on those things now. Daniel and I are off to town with the Quimby horses."

But as Father started off, Momma dropped Victory's hand, whirled on her husband, and spat out one terrible word.

Chapter 9

"WHISKEY!"

The kitchen reverberated. Momma leaned toward Father, fists on her hips. "Ashtabula will rue the day that that—*gentleman*—ever settled in Hoyle House. Never in my life—Clayton?—are you listening to me?" Momma asked fiercely.

"It's helping Homer, isn't it?" Father turned and faced her.

"Helping him?" Momma shrilled. "How can WHISKEY help anyone?" Father kept his face straight, but Victory saw sparks of humor flashing in his eyes.

"Sarah, I was just up in that room with our whiskey-besotted son, and what helps him I'm for, regardless of what it's called or what shape or color bottle it comes in. I'm thankful for young Simmons's skill. Miracle how he got that bullet out. . . ."

"You've said that a hundred times already." Momma flung out her arms as if to wave away the truth. "But WHISKEY. . . !"

"Sarah, be reasonable. I can't argue now because that new lake steamer docks at noon, and Daniel and I have a wagonload of cargo for it. I got word that the shipment is to go off in Bible barrels, so I want the usual food and water packed for those six barrels as quick as you can. Faith's coming with us. Less suspicious if there's a female along." He wheeled and went out.

Faith began packing the small jars and jugs that each slave would have with him in his barrel as Momma tied the bandage on Victory's burned hand. When Faith finished the six small bundles, she brought the coffee-pot and filled Momma's mug again. "Why do you hate the doctor today when you liked him yesterday?" she asked quietly.

"Daughter," Momma admitted, "I was uncordial, unQuaker, inhospitable; but—but—it's the whiskey. Whiskey is of the devil. What must the Good Lord be imagining, seeing those bottles up there?"

"Faith, hurry up," Father called, and Faith sprang out the back door with the food and water containers wrapped in her apron. Momma put the medicine box away, then she and Victory went up to Homer's room. Momma sank into the rocking chair by the bed, and Victory stood at the window watching the loading of the wagon.

One by one the Bible barrels came from the shed and were placed gently on a bed of straw on the wagon bed. There were thirteen in all—six filled with runaways; the other seven filled with real Bibles. Each long barrel was covered with a large shipping label to a Canadian port, then another label to an Indian village just above Lake Huron. Plastered over the wooden sides, painted in bold black letters, were the words: HOLY BIBLES. Then Father added several barrels of farm goods that he was shipping to Canada and some bags of grain for the mill. The Quimby horses were tied on behind. Father and Daniel inspected the loading, and satisfied, Father lifted Faith to the high wagon seat. Daniel sat on the tail end where he could watch the horses. Father sent his whip flicking out over Beauty and Molly, and the heavily-loaded wagon moved down the lane.

When Victory turned from the window, Momma was asleep. But Victory woke her, led her down to hers and Father's spacious bedroom, helped her out of her dress, and spread the dress across the back of one of the wing chairs on either side of the fireplace. Momma curled up on the wide bed. Victory covered her with a light blanket, pulled the shades, and tiptoed from the room.

Going into Homer's room, she leaned over his still body. An unfamiliar sweetish smell was on his breath. On the bedside table were four squat brown bottles. Whiskey—so that was what it smelled like? Opening one of the squat bottles, she took a whiff. It was the same. Sinking into the rocking chair, she held her bandaged hand, the left one, carefully in her lap. It hurt badly. If she'd been her usual self, she wouldn't have done such a stupid thing. She rocked a bit, but doing nothing made her uneasy. Getting up, she checked on Momma, then went down to the kitchen where she cleaned up the skillet and spilled batter. It took a long time with just one hand.

One hand—one leg.

Homer with only one leg. . . . In slow motion she put the teakettle on to heat water for the dishes. While she waited she went back up to check on Momma and Homer again. It took her an hour to clean up the kitchen, and her hand hurt more and more even though she tried to protect it. Finished at last, she knew that Father expected her to stay in the house, but just one quick look at the new foal wouldn't take more than a minute. Taking a handful of sugar from the bowl, she left the kitchen.

The foal was rushing about on its long, ungainly legs, sniffing, stopping to nurse, already alive to the world. Golden Dawn came at Victory's croon, and her soft lips lapped up the sugar in Victory's open palm. "My golden one." Victory felt her velvet nose. "I'll have to think of a name for your little one." Looking out at the exercise oval, she saw Peter astride Black Sir, one of Father's most valuable stallions. Victory wanted to stay here forever, watching her new foal, feeling the hot May sun on her face, being alone and idle, trying to forget. . . . Reluctantly she went back to the house. She looked in on Momma, then settled in the rocking chair in Homer's room. The longer she sat, the tighter a returning sense of guilt gripped her insides. Tears seeped down her cheeks as her mind went over and over every move in the woods. Shaking herself, she got up, got her diary, then made a second trip for the ink bottle and quill. Sinking into the rocker, she opened her diary. Yesterday's entry was incomplete. Picking up the quill she began to write, but it hurt to hold the diary. And the tightness in her mind made it almost impossible to concentrate. She wrote a sentence, then struck it out. A big blob of ink dropped onto her skirt. She tried again, and again crossed out the words. The tightness was a cramp all through her body. She looked over at Homer. He slept, his mouth wide open. Her eyes shifted to the squat bottles. ". . . whiskey-besotted son . . ."

Peace. Sleep.

And then something inside her, something she rarely let out, made her get up, go to the bedside table, unscrew the cap of one of the brown bottles, and pour a small glass to the brim. Putting it to her lips, she took a normal drink.

It were as if she'd swallowed the hot griddle handle—whole!

The blistering gulp slithered down her throat in a scalding waterfall. She choked and spluttered, but she didn't let go of the glass. It wasn't fair that Momma and Homer were asleep and she wasn't. She was sick too, with her burned hand. Sip. Sip. Sip. Her lips swelled slightly, but the firewater went down without taking her breath away again.

An invigorating feeling took hold of her. Lying back in the rocker, her mind came alive.

Nugget! Golden Dawn and Nugget. Setting the glass down, she reached for the diary.

May 14, 1852, Sixth Day
Nugget! The whiskey's done me good, just like Homer. Mustn't tell how I thought it up. Nugget. Nugget. Nugget. That's a perfect name. So glad I thought of it. . . .

Victory looked down at the page. Flies buzzed about the room. The exhilaration that she had felt vanished as quickly as it had come, and now it was hard to write in the diary

Nuget. Quill won't work. Can't write. Hand hurts.
Sleeppp

The glass of whiskey sat empty on the washstand.
The quill slipped from her hand, the diary slid from her
lap, and her head fell back against the soft cushion of
the rocker.

A slap woke her. Faith was standing there, looking at
her. "What's wrong with you, Victory?" Victory tried
to focus her eyes in her balloon-sized head. She pointed
to the glass. Faith left, and Victory closed her eyes
again. More sleep. But Faith was back forcing a mug of
coffee into her hands. "Drink—be quick." Victory
obeyed like a child while Faith gathered up the dropped
quill and diary. "They call me flighty and silly, but
you . . ." Faith said. "It's a good thing Father has lots
to unload." Then she giggled. "What's it like, Victory?
Dare I sneak a glass?"

"No," Victory said, struggling up out of the rocker
and standing unsteadily. Faith slapped her cheeks again,
hard. Then she pushed Victory's face and neck into a
basin of cold water. But the fog in Victory's huge head
didn't clear. Faith dried her twin's face and head.

"What's it taste like, Victory?" Faith asked again.

"Bed," Victory said. Faith led her to their room.
Victory fell across it, and the last thing she remembered
was Faith covering her with a blanket.

Chapter 10

Victory stirred and pulled her good hand across her eyes. Like a jigsaw puzzle, the pieces of the day fitted together. She edged off the bed and went to the mantel. There sat the ink bottle, quill, and her diary. Good Faith. Locking her secret book away, she went slowly out into the hall. She felt as if she were made of glass. Hanging onto the back stairs handrail, she went down, through the deserted kitchen, and out onto the back porch. And there she stood, hugging herself, for the wind had a sharp edge to it. Father came out of the carriage shed, and seeing her, came striding across the barnyard. "Feeling better, daughter? Faith said you were ill."

"Fine now."

"Sarah, Homer . . . ?"

"Both sleeping. Did the shipment get off, Father?"

"Like clockwork. Luke's with it."

"Skinhead?"

"No more questions now. Begin supper, lame as you are. I don't want your mother wakened."

"Where's Faith?"

"Below—cleaning. Soon as it's dark, I'm fixing to open. . . ." He stopped himself. "More at supper, daughter, when the windows and doors are closed." He turned and headed for the shed.

Victory drew in great breaths of the chill air. She felt less brittle all the time. Returning to the kitchen, she began supper. There were footsteps on the back stairs. "Momma," Victory said. "You're up."

"Pure sloth—sleeping the day away," Momma said, taking her apron from behind the door. "Homer's awake, and I just asked him if he wanted something to drink or eat, but he said no. You run up, Victory. He might take something if you asked him."

Victory went up. "Homer, it's me," she said. "How're you feeling?" Homer muttered something she didn't understand and rolled his head away from her. "Homer, want something to drink?" He shook his head. "Not anything—not even honey tea?"

"Honey tea?" Homer's face rolled back toward her. "Say, sis, that'd taste good. Could you make me some?"

"Could I?" Victory flew from the room.

"Honey tea, Momma," Victory said triumphantly.

"You and Homer." Momma just smiled as she began to make the tea. Later as Victory climbed the stairs, the mug of tea in her good hand, it hurt to hold up her skirts, but Momma was too busy getting supper to remember the burned hand.

"Here, Homer." She put her arm behind his head and lifted so he could swallow. When the mug was empty, Homer asked for a second. Victory got it for him.

"Why's your hand bandaged, Victory?" Homer asked.

"Burned it on the griddle handle."

"That wasn't very smart," he said. "But then I wasn't so smart with Skinhead. Shouldn't have riled him like I did. Made big trouble for everyone." His face was flushed by the hot tea, and the restless head-turning of the first night returned. Victory reached for the whiskey bottle. She didn't know the correct dosage, but she poured the glass half-full and put it to Homer's lips. He gulped it down. "More," he said. "Know what that is, Victory?"

"Yes."

"Knocks me out. It's only then I don't. . . ." He stopped.

". . . feel your leg." Victory finished for him. The tightness that had gone when she'd been drunk and asleep now returned worse than ever.

A stiffening wind pushed at the house, and Victory went to the window. "Storm coming," she said, fighting the tightness. Finally she turned and went back to the bed. Homer's eyes were glazed over, so she pulled the blinds and went back down to the kitchen.

Chapter 11

"Wasted day," Father said, after they looked up from their silent grace about the supper table. "No one I talked to mentioned the shooting, so the doctor's kept his word. We delivered the Quimby horses, then went to the dock. Luke was there, and he took charge of the Canadian shipment. Left the grain at the mill, then started looking for Skinhead and his two cronies, but nary hide nor hair of them could we find. A body can't go around shooting people no matter how thick he is with the local constable. Next we went to Miller's General Store. Big new poster up about runaways from MarbleHall in Kentucky. Brian Owen-Smith and Asa Pennypacker were talking up a storm about the poster with Orville Miller. They all wanted my opinion, but I just did your shopping, Sarah, and we came home."

Wind-driven rain rattled on the windows, and the lanterns flickered in the drafts. Father wiped his beard and rose. "That cave's a stink hole, so we're going to pull as much of this storm wind down the Liberty Well and through the labyrinth as we can. Means guarding, even though the cave's empty. Peter, open everything up, and you and White sit in the wardrobe room by the trapdoor. Daniel, take Blueboy and open the riverbank entrance. Paul and I'll relieve you at midnight." He turned on his heel and headed out into the wet darkness, Daniel and Peter following.

Paul got up and without even a good-night to Momma, stomped up the stairs to bed. Momma sighed after him and shook her head hopelessly. "Victory, go ask Homer if he'll eat anything?"

"He's asleep," Victory said. "He wanted his whiskey after the honey tea, and I gave it to him." Momma frowned and was about to say something when stones rattled against the kitchen window that looked out over the side porch. Faith flew to the dining room door and returned with five runaways—three females and a man carrying a small child.

Victory stared at their soaked clothes, their chapped hands, the man's bare feet. "He said," Faith pointed to the lone man, "that they came from TROUT SOUTH."

"Welcome to ERIE SHORES," Momma said. "Faith get towels, clothes, and blankets and put them in your room. They'll change up there."

The shivering bedraggled group edged up to the hot range, and their wet clothes steamed. Momma warmed milk for the little girl and poured coffee for the four adults. Faith was back in a trice. "Everything's ready, Momma," she said.

"If you'll go with my daughter, she'll show you where you can change. Take the teakettle, Faith, so they'll have hot water." The blacks followed Faith who was carrying the teakettle. When she returned, the three women began preparing supper for the new shipment.

68

"A night for witches and goblins," Father said as he came in, shedding his rain covering. Momma told him about the runaways. He nodded, not surprised. He and Momma talked in low tones for a few minutes while Victory and Faith got the table ready.

Soon the back stairs door opened slowly, and the youngest black woman, carrying a candle, peered into the kitchen. "Come, sit, food's ready," Father said. The blacks came in, dressed in dry clothes, with blankets wrapped about their shoulders like shawls. The man still carried the little girl.

"There," Momma said, putting a brimming plate before each of the adults. "Eat hearty now, and then there'll be a safe, dry, warm place for you to sleep." The runaways began to eat, the man feeding his daughter from his own plate. Momma put another glass of warm milk next to his coffee cup and smiled down at the child. Father went out to tell Daniel and Peter of the new arrivals.

"I'm Zeke," the man said, "'n this here be mah woman, Clovis, 'n mah mammy, LuBelle, 'n mah granny, Louisiana, 'n mah young'un, Lily."

"Where're you from?" Momma asked.

"Tennessee. Massa Lodge, he finally dies after years 'n years 'n we was scared we be sold away. . . ."

"So you ran before that could happen?" Faith asked, nodding. "Smart."

"We was terrible lucky," Zeke said. "Peddlar man he come 'n help us git away. He hides us in his wagon the day of Massa Lodge's funeral. They miss us pretty soon, 'n come high-tailin' after us, but that peddlar man, he gits us safe to a house where we hides—just in time. 'N they never 'spect him—not that dumb ole peddlar man."

"Was that the only time you were chased?" Momma asked.

"Yas'm."

"How long've you been on the road?" Faith asked.

"Long, long time," Zeke said. "Louisiana, she plum tuckered out."

"Y'all watch your mouth." Louisiana shot her grandson a sharp, alert look. "'Twas me says to run. We the only slaves on that plantation with such long line unbroke."

"We close to Canada?" Zeke asked.

"Very close," Momma replied. "Just sent six off today by—" She stopped knowing she shouldn't reveal the means of escape. "And by now they're in Canada—free men."

"Free men. . . ."

". . . 'n women," Louisiana said loudly, pointing a finger at herself. "Women free like men. No more bull slaves with snake whips a'leerin' at the gals. My Lily, she gonna grow up like the ladies in the plantation house—with manners 'n learnin' 'n all them things."

"When we goin' on?" Zeke leaned forward.

"With the Good Lord's help, you'll be Under The Lion's Paw before the moon is full." Momma smiled.

"Praise the Lord. Free at last." Louisiana folded her hands and looked at the ceiling.

Victory watched her. Freedom? What would it be like to step onto the shores of Canada and have freedom fall down on you all in a heap? What was freedom anyway? What was being a slave?

Lily slid from her father's lap and began undoing the

buttons at the top of the dress that Faith had given her. From beneath the high neck she pulled out a dirty string and the object that it held. "Dolly," she said. Momma and Faith leaned forward, and Victory moved to the vacant chair beside Zeke.

"It's—it's so different," Victory said.

"Not dolly," Louisiana said. "Charm. My mammy give it to me when I be a young'un like Lily here. I give it to LuBelle 'n she give it to Zeke 'n now Lily got it. That there thing come from Africa 'round my mammy's neck."

"What kind of charm is it?" Momma asked.

"Keep off the evil spirits 'n the sicknesses." Now Momma and Faith came over to look more closely at the figure. It was carved from some dark wood and was worn to a sheen from the skin it had rubbed against for generations. It was the figure of a woman about four inches high and two inches wide. The legs and arms were squat and straight, the body short with a distended stomach, but the head sat on a long graceful neck. The figure's hair was piled into a high V, and waves were carved into the headdress. The face was simply carved —just holes for eyes, a slit for a mouth, and a raised broad nose. The ear on the left side was missing, but from the right ear dangled a small golden earring.

"My dolly," Lily repeated. Both Victory and Momma felt the satin finish of the figure and turned it over and over, taking in every detail. "Hurt hand?" Lily pointed to Victory's bandage.

"Yes. You see, I had no dolly-charm to help me." Victory smiled, and Lily's face lit up like a sunset.

A commotion on the back porch made the blacks

71

freeze. As the door opened, the wind almost blew the lanterns out, and the fire in the range flared up. Peter and Father leaned against the heavy door to close it. They stood dripping, taking in the serene scene before them.

"Where're they sleeping?" Peter asked.

"Barn."

"Why not the cave?" Peter asked. "We're already guarding it."

"Too drafty. Peter and Faith, out to the wardrobe room and fill a trunk with things they'll need in the haymow," Father said. "Peter and I'll carry it to the barn when it's ready." Then Father knelt by Lily. As Lily held out her doll for him to look at, the rotted string broke. Momma got up to get more string, but Father said, "I took the ball to the carriage shed this morning, Sarah. We'll tie the doll up tomorrow."

Faith returned. "All set, Father."

"Come, all of you," Father said. Zeke got up, picked up Lily, who clutched her dolly in her hand, and the three women followed. Momma went up to check on Homer.

"So," Faith said, "five more for your diary, Victory. That makes eleven this week. That doll-charm—imagine believing it can scare away illnesses and evil spirits! Victory, you haven't asked me what happened in town today. Do you want to hear?" Victory nodded. "Well," Faith began, "guess who I saw?"

"Who?" But Victory's response was automatic, for her mind was split—half listening to Faith, half thinking of the barn.

What on earth could be taking them so long?

Chapter 12

"Louise and her mother, that's who, at Miller's. Mr. Miller had some new summer bonnets, and there was one pink one, all tucks and ribbons, that looked just perfect on Louise." Faith laughed softly. "It looked perfect on me too."

"Did Father see you?"

"No, 'cause he was looking at a big new poster about runaways; and Mr. Pennypacker, Mr. Owen-Smith and even Mr. Miller were all talking to him about it."

"It must have been the MarbleHall runaway's poster," Victory said, "that Father told us about before. Remember?" But Faith, who was afraid of horses and didn't know why MarbleHall was so important, went rattling on.

"Louise bought two bonnets and slave cotton cambric to make dresses to match. Victory, why couldn't we be Methodists like the Quimbys? Think what it would be like, sashaying into Meeting looking like a spring bouquet instead of a dead stick."

But by now Victory wasn't listening. She got up and flung her cloak over her head with her one good hand.

"Where're you going?" Faith asked.

"To see why they haven't come back." Faith was on her feet at once, and they left the house together. As they came near the barn, the wavering light of a lantern bobbed about. Peter was bent over, holding the lantern close to the puddles, searching. "What in the world. . . ?" The wind whipped the words from Victory's mouth.

"That blankety-blank kid dropped her blankety-blank dolly between here and the haymow somewhere. Just hope it hasn't floated out the lane by now." Faith stayed with Peter to help him, but Victory slipped through the barely open barn doors. Childish crying echoed to the rafters. Victory's skin crawled. She rounded the corner, and there was Zeke with another lantern, searching the straw-littered corridor.

"Poor Lily," Victory said. Zeke jumped and whirled to see who had crept up on him.

"Yas'm. She ain't stopped hollerin' since she lost that dolly. That charm—it done brung us luck all these years —'n now it's gone—puff. Bad thing."

"No," Victory tried to assure him. "It's not a bad thing. We'll find it, you wait and see." Zeke gave her an unbelieving look and turned back to his search. Victory thought a minute, then splashed back to the house and pulled a small trunk from beneath the big double bed where she and Faith slept. She took out a rag doll and stuck it under her arm. On her way out, she stopped in Homer's room. Momma was knitting and rocking.

"Lily lost her doll-charm, and she's yelling her head off, so I'm going to give her my rag doll." Momma just nodded. Victory drew her cloak about her again and fighting the fierce wind, waded back to the barn. Peter, Faith, and Zeke all had given up their searching and were in the haymow corner. Victory gave the doll to Clovis. Clovis pressed it into her daughter's arms, but Lily threw it away and kept right on screaming. Clovis and Zeke exchanged despairing glances.

"Let her cry," Victory said. "No one's going to hear her over this storm, and she'll cry herself to sleep."

"But what about the morning?" Faith asked. "The doctor's—"

"Never mind about that," Peter said quickly. "You twins, take this lantern back to the house." Then turning to the runaways he said, "Zeke, stay here in the mow no matter what you hear or suspect. Before dawn tomorrow we'll move you to a safe place where Lily can scream her lungs out and no one except the devil will hear her. Two of us, with dogs, will be on guard all night." He dumped the contents of the trunk into the hay. "Now change and get some sleep." He took the lantern from Zeke, while the runaways sorted out what they needed. Faith and Victory went slowly down the haymow ladder, Lily's screams still in their ears. They sloshed to the house, went to their bedroom, got dry and into their night clothes, then went to Homer's room. A candle glowed, Momma knitted, and Homer snored.

It wasn't long before Father stuck his head in the door and said softly, "Sarah, can't we go down to the kitchen to talk as soon as I get dried out?" Momma nodded yes.

"Some storm," Father said as he came in a few minutes later, dressed for guarding. Momma put a cup of coffee before him. "At least one good thing's coming out of tonight—the air in the cave is breathable again."

"But what about Lily's doll?" Faith asked.

"Paul and I'll look for it when we go out to relieve Daniel and Peter." At the mention of his name, Paul came down and Momma gave him coffee also. Father filled him in on what had happened since supper.

"These the MarbleHall runaways?" Paul leaned forward.

"No, just ordinary runaways," Father said. Paul fell back in his chair, his disappointment showing in his face.

"MarbleHall," Paul said. "Thoroughbreds, race tracks, slaves to look after everything—must be heaven. . . ." He broke off. "How many got away?" Father held up one calloused hand, his fingers and thumb spread wide.

"The likes of what?"

"Three jockeys and two trainers."

"I'd give my right arm to see MarbleHall," Paul said. "Wonder how Black Sir or Gretchen Girl would stand up against some of MarbleHall's best?"

"That would be some race." Father couldn't keep the eagerness out of his voice.

"What is MarbleHall anyway?" Faith asked impatiently.

"The most famous horse plantation in Kentucky—maybe the whole south," Father said. "If you were as interested in horseflesh as Victory is and not so much in dogs and bonnets, then you wouldn't be asking. To bed with you two." Father waved the twins upstairs. "We've got a very early morning tomorrow, if we're going to get those runaways down into the cave before Doctor Simmons gets here."

The twins rose, kissed Momma good night and went to their room. They crawled into the cold bed and snuggled to get warm. Faith was soon asleep, but for the first time, Victory began to worry about the shipment. That, on top of the tenseness she had felt since Homer's shooting, kept her awake. Those fugitives in the barn? Slaves? To her slavery meant never sleeping in a clean wide bed, never waking to the smell of perking coffee in a lamp-lit kitchen, never having any real leisure, never knowing when you'd be sold away from those you loved, never reading. . . . "Oh, Lord, why was I so lucky to not be born a slave? Bless the slaves and Homer and everyone. Forgive me my sins. Amen."

Chapter 13

The clock bonged four times as Victory came into the kitchen.

"You've got a sixth sense about time." Father grinned at her. "How's your hand?"

"Fine," Victory lied, for it still hurt very much. Momma closed the lid on the last of the four hampers, and Father put them into a shapeless sack.

"I'm going to stow this in the shed, then go get Zeke. If you go out, keep your eyes peeled for that doll."

Victory and Momma stood at the door watching. The storm was over, and the barnyard was no longer completely covered with water. Dawn was an hour away. Soon Father came from the barn, Zeke behind him carrying the still-sleeping Lily, the three women following, holding their long skirts up out of the water and muck. Father saw them all into the shed, and the doors closed behind them. Momma breathed a sigh of relief. "Wish we'd find that doll," she said. "Then I'd rest easy."

Faith came down, rubbing her eyes. "Victory," Momma said, "take the lantern and go look. You can't help much here with just one hand." Victory put on her cloak, picked up the lantern, and went out into the swimming barnyard. She bent double, looking, looking, but found nothing. When Paul and Father came out of the carriage shed, they chained Blueboy to his dog-house and ordered Redgirl and White to the porch. Victory ceased her searching and went in to eat break-fast with them.

Nobody talked. Victory thought about Nugget, but even that didn't lift her spirits. She knew she should tell the family that she'd decided on a name for her foal, but somehow this wasn't the right time. After breakfast, when Father and Paul had left for the barn, Momma said, "Victory, you can gather eggs with that lame hand." Again Victory put on her cloak and went out, her eyes on the ground, searching, searching, until at last she reached the hen house. The sluggish hens hardly moved as she pushed her hand under them. Gathering up her apron, she filled it with eggs. As she left, she kicked the door closed with her foot and latched it with her good hand. Dawn was brushing the eastern sky, the clouds turning scarlet, when she turned toward the house, eyes again on the ground; but Blueboy began to growl and she looked up.

There, coming up the lane, was the doctor. The mud had muffled his horse's hoofbeats so only Blueboy had heard them.

"You keep your word, don't you, Doctor Simmons," she called loudly, hoping Momma—everyone—would hear her.

"I try, Victory," the doctor called back to her. The horse moved across the swampy barnyard toward her, and she grasped the reins with her good hand. "Are you always at your chores at dawn?" he asked. "Or is it that foal of yours that's gotten you up so early?"

"Both," Victory answered.

"Come, Victory." He dismounted quickly, untied her apron, took the eggs and laid them carefully beside the hen house, saying, "We'll steal a minute to look at your foal before we go in."

Victory hesitated, but she couldn't think of any reason to refuse his suggestion. He remounted, leaned down, swept her up, and settled her before him in the saddle. They rode to the stables, where Victory slid down and the doctor dismounted and opened the doors. He tied the reins of his horse to the gate of an empty stall.

Their time alone with Golden Dawn and the foal was short, for Father came in almost at once. "Welcome, Doctor. Victory's got such a puffed-up head about that foal that she's dragged you out here before she even brings you into the house as a properly reared daughter should."

"Don't blame her, Clayton," the doctor said. "It's my fault."

"Take the doctor in, Victory, while I tend to his horse," Father said. Victory and the doctor set out across the muddy barnyard.

"How's your hand, Victory?"

"Fine."

"Quite a cyclone we had last night, wasn't it?" the doctor went on, swinging his black bag. "And how has Homer been since I left him yesterday?"

"Better."

"Did he take . . . ?"

80

"He had honey tea," Victory said, "and. . . ."

The doctor had stopped, and with the toe of his boot touched something floating in a puddle. He bent down and scooped it up in one swift motion. There, in his palm, lay Lily's doll-charm. Victory's heart stopped beating as he rubbed the strange wooden figure against his trousers to dry it, then slipped it into his coat pocket without comment.

". . . whiskey," Victory finished, her voice steady, her face a smiling mask of unconcern about what the doctor had just found. They reached the porch and stamped as much of the mud and water from their feet as they could. Momma opened the kitchen door.

"Doctor Simmons—Homer's *waiting*." Her voice was frigid. "Victory, where're those eggs?" She turned and went back to the hen house.

Father came from the stables, and she motioned him to her, whispering, "The doctor. He found Lily's doll-charm, and it's in his coat pocket this minute."

Father's worry wrinkles creased his nose.

"Damn!" he said.

Victory almost dropped her egg-filled apron. Father never swore!

Chapter 14

As they stepped inside, Victory's eyes swept the kitchen while Father went up to Homer's room. "Where's the doctor's coat, Faith?"

"I hung it on the hall rack—why?"

"Nothing," Victory said as she went to the large coat and hat rack that filled half the downstairs hall. She slipped her good hand into both pockets. Both were empty.

He still had it!

She sank down on the hat rack seat, troubled and upset. But it wouldn't do to show it, so finally she returned to the kitchen. Faith hadn't missed her, for she was standing at the back stairs door, listening.

"So the danger of infection is passed, and the wound is healing?" Father's voice asked. "That's mighty good news, Doctor. Come, have a spot of breakfast with us to celebrate."

"No breakfast," the doctor replied as he came down the stairs, "but I'll have a cup of that head-clearing coffee of Sarah's." Faith ran to the stove, filled three mugs, and set them before her parents and the doctor as they sat down at the table.

Momma perched on the edge of her chair, and in a moment picked up her cup, barely nodded to the doctor, and said, "I'm going back to Homer."

"Good day, Sarah." The doctor got to his feet and bowed to her stiff back as she stalked up the stairs. "Ashtabula's quite a leaping-off place for runaway slaves, isn't it, Clayton?" Doctor Simmons said out of the blue.

"All these lake ports are," Father said.

"In Baltimore all the Quakers I knew were abolitionists—and into this Underground Railroad thing. You heard about that, Clayton?"

"Underground Railroad?" Victory trembled as Father looked the doctor straight in the eye. "Who hasn't heard about it? I read the paper, see the posters, hear the rumors about runaways heading across the lake for Canada, but I never have seen one running, so there must be an underground something-or-other. The way I see it, Doctor, is this. A man breaks his back earning a living, and if he's lucky, he accumulates some property. I'm a Quaker, true—but if a horse thief made off with Golden Dawn's foal, I'd have Constable Gilly out here so fast it would make your head swivel."

"Have you ever seen runaways that have been caught here being returned south?" the doctor asked.

"Everybody has. And everybody's heard Constable Gilly brag about how he catches more runaways every year."

"But some must slip through?" the doctor insisted.

"None of my business." Father shook his head. "I mind my own business, and I expect others to do the same."

"Except for that fellow who shot Homer," the doctor

said. Father's head snapped up. "Don't you worry, I'll deal with him when I catch him."

"Well." The doctor rose. "Clayton, your boy's over the hump. No need for me to stop again, but if there's an emergency, of course, I'll come at once. Now, my coat. Where'd you hide it, Faith?"

She ran to get it and held it as he slipped his arms into it. Then she handed him his black bag, and he smiled and patted her shoulder in thanks. Faith beamed and went out with him as he and Father went to the porch.

Victory didn't move out of her chair. Her fear made it hard for her to breathe.

Chapter 15

Faith came back in, sighing. "That Doctor Simmons—I wish he'd come every single day."

"He just may," Victory said.

"What do you mean by that?" Faith asked.

"He found the doll-charm."

"Where!" Faith demanded.

"Floating in a puddle," Victory said. "I searched his coat pockets, but it wasn't there, so he's still got it. Now he's got positive proof that this *is* an Underground Railroad station. That's why he asked Father all those questions."

"But he wouldn't give us away—would he, Victory?" Faith's voice quavered. "He'll keep it a secret just like he did about Homer's leg, won't he?"

"Then why did he keep the doll? It was on our property, that means it was ours, but he kept it and hid it." Just then Momma came down the stairs, and they explained everything to her, including the fact that Victory had already told Father.

"Trouble by the bushel," Momma said too seriously. "That doll-charm could end this station today. But," she brightened, "the real evidence is the *shipment,* so the sooner we get rid of them, the better. Faith, run find your father."

When Father and Faith returned, Father put his arm about Momma. "The shipment's already out the riverbank exit and on its way to TREE WEST."

"Thank the Lord," Momma said. "But who's leading them?"

"Lilac," Father said. "She was on her way over here to see Victory and the new foal, so I turned her about with the fugitives."

"So now it's his word against ours that he found that strange looking thing here in our barnyard?"

"Right." Father paused as Daniel and Peter came down. They had slept late because of their night guarding. Father told them in a few words what had happened. "Get some breakfast into you, then Daniel, to the smithy, and Peter, take over exercising the horses from Paul. He's bushed and hungry, and he'll eat and go right to bed when he comes in."

Victory looked at Father. Often he'd been up two nights in a row, guarding or bringing in a shipment, but he never slept in the daytime. It was *his* station, and she knew he'd protect it with his life. He and King had found the cave when they had been drilling a water well. It was exactly like the caves that were out in the lake bluffs, but no one in town or on the farms about had drilled into it, so it was a perfect secret. Father believed that the cave had been divinely revealed to him, and to him alone, so that he could fight slavery, which he hated with all his soul. And once Father was convinced the Inner Voice had spoken to him, nothing—

neither the fear of imprisonment nor death—could sway him. It was the Lord's cave, and Father and King were His agents. Two hundred and thirty-four runaways had passed through the cave in just three years. Victory knew because she had it recorded in her diary. How many King and Father had spirited through before that, she didn't know.

"I'm going out to do what I can to scramble the trail of that shipment; and Daniel and Peter, once you've eaten, come help me. Sarah, scrub in here as you usually do. Then if the doctor and honorable Constable Gilly pay us a visit, we'll be ready for them." He went out.

Faith went to get the scrub buckets, and Victory looked down at her bandaged hand. Momma saw the look and said, "Go ask Homer what he wants for breakfast besides honey tea."

Victory sprang up the stairs and into Homer's room. His eyelids were thick and red, but he grinned up at her. "How're you feeling, Homer?"

"Rotten," he said, but the grin remained.

"Oh, Homer, I didn't mean to get you shot, honest I didn't."

"Get me shot?" He laughed. "Your scream most likely kept me out of Skinhead's squirrely stew."

"You really think that, Homer?"

"Sure do. No scream—no Homer," he joked. And with that something seemed to let go inside of Victory. She'd heard it from Homer himself, and for the first time, she believed.

"What do you want for breakfast?" she asked happily.

"Custard, two pieces of pie, and honey tea." Victory

was almost out of the room when she turned back.

"Golden Dawn had her foal, Homer, and guess what I've named it?"

"I give up." Homer waved his hands impatiently. "Tell me."

"Nugget." Victory didn't wait for his reaction but darted down the stairs.

"Nugget," she shouted as she burst into the kitchen. "Nugget, out of Golden Dawn."

"Good name," Peter said. Daniel shrugged his approval. Momma made up Homer's tray and carried it up herself. Daniel and Peter left. It had begun to rain again—the scarlet dawn had been a false omen of good weather.

Faith was on her knees, scrubbing everything in sight, and Victory began to clear the table. "You think this is the end of the station, Victory?" Faith asked.

"Depends on what the doctor does with the doll-charm."

"What *will* he do with it?"

"I wish I knew, Faith. We'll just have to wait and see."

"Wait—wait—wait," Faith cried, rearing up on her knees. "Me, I'm waiting to get off this awful farm and to the city like Isaac or to California like Joshua."

Victory didn't answer. She finished clearing the table, then went upstairs, leaving Faith storming about the kitchen. She got out her diary.

May 15, 1852, Seventh Day
　　Diary, this may be the last entry I'll write. I'm going to hide you in one of the boxes in the laby-

rinth. You, precious diary, would send us all to prison—if the doll-charm doesn't first.

Victory got up, wrapped the diary in a piece of red velvet that Louise had given to Faith, and put it in the band of her skirt. Down the front stairs and out the door into the rain she went, over to the carriage shed. In a minute she was through the secret panel and into the Liberty Well. It took a long time to unlock the door with only one hand, but finally she kicked the stones against it and made sure the door was fast. Taking a candle, she went through the big cave to the concealed opening in the far wall and entered the labyrinth. She knew her way by heart, and when she came to the last box that Father had put in the tunnels to point directions, she put the diary in that box. Hurrying, she retraced her steps and was back in her room before she was missed. Quickly she changed into dry clothes and began to think about what she'd take to prison with her.

Chapter 16

Thirteen!

This coming Seventh Day was Victory's and Faith's birthday. All the guests had been invited for the noon meal, and Victory could hardly wait.

Then Momma started itching.

Two weeks had passed since the doctor had found the doll-charm, but so far he'd done nothing. As each day passed, Victory's thoughts of prison faded, and she even wondered if she shouldn't go get her diary from the labyrinth. Only one shipment had gone through, but several days after they left, Momma got a patch of brownish rash on her back. It itched, and none of her homemade remedies helped. Father had asked Clarasue to look at it, and she had said at once, "Jumbo fever."

"What's that?" Father had asked.

"Southern thing. It's a wonder none of us has gotten it from all the slaves we've sent through here. It ain't deadly, comes on a body slowly—first you just itch and have a little fever, but then, overnight, the rash spreads, the fever goes higher than a kite, you cough up your insides, and the rash oozes pus. I had it once, and it makes a body feel just turrible, but it goes away in time."

Momma pretended she didn't itch, but Victory knew the rash was there even though it hadn't started to spread. The only outward sign of the fever showed in Momma's flushed face. But she had insisted on coming to town this morning in the wagon with Father, Faith, and Victory to do some special shopping for the party. Faith hovered by Momma as she made her purchases, but Victory stared up at the MarbleHall poster. Father had gone to do some other errands.

REWARD—REWARD—REWARD

FOR INFORMATION OR RETURN OF STOLEN PROPERTIES

Five black male slaves, belonging to Colonel Calhoun Pettybone, were kidnapped—AGAINST THEIR WILL—from MarbleHall Plantation, Lexington, Kentucky, on Saturday night, May 1, 1852. All are expert horse handlers. Two are trainers of carriage horses and three are racing jockeys.

A REWARD of 1,000 gold dollars shall be paid to any person or persons giving information about the kidnappers of these slaves.

A REWARD of 2,000 gold dollars *per slave* shall be paid to any person or persons who actually catches any of this kidnapped property.

DESCRIPTIONS OF THE SLAVES

Bull Coffee-with-cream colored, shaven head, scar running from left ear down neck to left shoulder blade.

Height: six feet, three inches
Weight: 220 pounds
Horse trainer and groom

Black Jack Copper colored, gray woolly hair, crooked left ankle so walks with limp.
Height: six feet, two inches
Weight: 180 pounds
Horse trainer and groom.

Scipo Burnt-gingerbread colored, shaven head, no eyebrows, little finger missing on right hand.
Height: five feet, two inches
Weight: 106 pounds
Jockey

Brutus Chestnut colored, shaven head, three upper front teeth missing, very small head.
Height: five feet and zero inches
Weight: 100 pounds
Jockey.

Cato Coal black, gray hair, wrinkled.
Height: four feet, ten inches
Weight: 90 pounds
Jockey

Anyone who knows the whereabouts of these kidnapped slaves, report it to your local constable so that these law enforcement officers can return these victims to their rightful owner and have the kidnappers jailed and prosecuted as the law of the land demands.

Victory shook her head. Colonel Calhoun Pettybone must be some kind of madman to think his slaves weren't just ordinary runaways. AGAINST THEIR WILL, indeed, why. . . .

"That will be all, Mr. Miller," Momma said brusquely. The storekeeper's pale hands wrapped the last items and placed them gently in the box where Momma's other purchases were stacked.

"Anything else, Mrs. Strawbridge, anything at all?" he said in that toadying voice of his.

"No thank you, Mr. Miller," she said. "Victory, Faith. . . ."

Suddenly there was a shout, and a wagon went hurtling down the street. They all ran out onto the boardwalk.

There was a great commotion before Constable Gilly's office. Wagons and carts mingled with the large group of men in the street. Victory saw Father's Quaker hat towering over the crowd.

Just then the door of Constable Gilly's office opened, and the Constable emerged holding a stout chain and pulling after him a black man whose arms were tied securely behind him. Deputy Weed came on their heels, leading two black women similarly bound with stout rope and chained. The crowd rumbled but parted as the two officers shoved their prisoners off the plank walk so viciously that the black man fell. One of the men in the crowd stepped forward and confronted the Constable. "Haven't gotta rub his face in the dirt, do yah, Gilly? Ain't yah pleasured yourself 'nough catchin' these runaways even though they ain't those fancy Pettybone ones?" He bent down to help the black man to his feet.

"What're yah gonna do with the reward money,

Gilly?" came an anonymous voice. The crowd took up the chant. "Reward money, reward money."

"Git!" squealed Gilly. "You're obstructin' justice 'n disturbin' the peace, 'n I'll arrest the lot of yah if yah doesn't—"

"Why, Constable, we'd bulge your precious little jail all outa shape." The crowd laughed. Several men moved toward Gilly.

The Constable drew his gun and waved it at the approaching men. "I say *git,* 'n I's—gonna—shoot—the—first—man—who—comes—toward—these—here—prisoners." The men edged back, and the crowd regrouped in clumps, muttering and eyeing Gilly and Weed as they chained the blacks to a closed carriage that was standing beside the jail. As soon as the captives were secure, two men emerged from inside the carriage; one loosened the reins from the hitching railing, then both climbed quickly to the driver's seat. The driver gave the team a crack with his whip, and the carriage moved out fast down Main Street, scattering the crowd. Victory saw two rifles on the footboard below the driver's feet as the carriage came by. Then came the captives, resigned agony on their faces, running to keep up with the horses' pace.

Victory's face went ashen. Once before she'd seen slaves taken away, but they had been put in a wagon and driven away. These three—running behind the carriage like animals. . . .

"They'll run 'em like that the whole way back to Virginny," said Mr. Miller. "Teach 'em a lesson and set an example for other slaves along the way to see. It's a fair step to Virginny from here."

"Oh!" Victory doubled both hands into fists. "I wish I were a *man*. I'd rescue them. I wouldn't let that Silly Gilly and Greedy Weedy get away with—"

"Hush your mouth," Momma snapped.

"Now, Miss Victory," said Mr. Miller. "The tales the abolitionists tell 'round here, you'd think every slave leads a horrible life, but it just ain't so. They're contented being looked after."

"Then why do they run away if they're so contented?" Victory whirled on Mr. Miller before Momma could stop her. Father came striding up just then, and Mr. Miller vanished into his store.

"So you saw?" Father said. Momma nodded. Father silently loaded the provisions into the wagon, then lifted Momma to the high seat in front beside him. She pulled her bonnet veil down to hide her red face. The girls climbed into the back, sobered and angry.

Victory looked up at Hoyle House, high on its promontory above the lake and town. She saw the telescope turned toward the lake on its stand in one round tower; the spyglass turned inland in the second tower. Had the doctor helped Gilly catch those slaves? And what had he done with the doll-charm?

They were almost home, the team going at a fast trot, when the wagon slowed and moved out of the middle of the pike. "Good day, Sarah and Clayton." Faith and Victory stood up in the barely moving wagon at Doctor Simmons's hail. This was the first time they had seen him since the doll-charm incident.

"Good day, yourself, Doctor," Father replied. "That's a mighty handsome piece of horseflesh you have stepping out before that *new* gig."

"Thank you, Clayton," the doctor said. "Bought this outfit in Cleveland not long ago." Victory saw him give Father a piercing look. "I'm in the market now for a matched pair of carriage horses, and I haven't time to return to Cleveland. Think you might have something for me?" Father hesitated. Momma sat still as a rabbit beside him, her veil covering her face.

"Might," Father said, then he blurted out. "We're having a birthday party for the twins this coming Seventh Day. Could you come for the noon meal with us?" Victory heard Faith suck in her breath.

The doctor half rose in his seat and bowed. "Congratulations, Victory and Faith. Clayton, I accept your kind invitation. How's Homer?"

"Up and walking," Father said.

"And your hand, Victory?"

"Healed, thank you." Victory held it out.

"Your mother's a good nurse. Well, I must be on my way. Till Seventh Day." He lifted his hat and was gone. Victory heard Momma sniff under her veil as Father started the team. She hadn't mentioned the doctor's name since the whiskey and doll-charm incidents. Victory had had to bury three full whiskey bottles once Homer had recovered enough not to need them.

When the wagon pulled into the barnyard, the twins jumped off and raced upstairs to change out of their town clothes. Faith was dressed and gone in a minute, and Victory was just behind when she happened to glance out the west window that looked down the U drive to a clump of trees along the pike. A figure came from that cluster of trees. It was Father. She watched him stride up the drive and out of sight.

Odd. The word settled in Victory's mind, unbidden.

"Victory?" Momma's angry voice came up the stairs. "Get down here." Victory sighed and went. She knew she'd have to listen to Momma's tirade against the doctor and Father's impulsive invitation.

Chapter 17

All the guests but the doctor had arrived: the Quimbys and Louise; the McNeals and two small sons, Steven and Charles; the Hathaways and their three daughters, Marie, Mary, and Margaret; the Owen-Smiths and their son, Lloyd, and daughter, Greta; and the Pennypackers, who had no children, but who were the Strawbridge's nearest neighbors. The men sat on the porch railing, and the women rocked in chairs brought from the house. The heat was smothering, and the women fanned themselves.

Faith and all her friends giggled and joked under the big birch tree by the drive, while Victory stood apart, talking with Mary Hathaway. Everyone looked up as the doctor drove down the long U drive in his new gig. "Happy birthday, Faith," called the doctor as he pulled on the reins. "Come, I'll give you a birthday twirl." Faith clambered into the gig and away they went, up past the porch of clapping and cheering adults and down the other side of the drive. They went around twice, Faith waving and bowing like a princess. Then the doctor stopped by Victory and Mary. "Your turn, Victory." She got in and had her two rounds with the doctor. After that he took all the other girls for a ride—but only once around the drive. Today was special for the twins. When the rides were over, the doctor joined the men while Peter led the gig away and stabled the doctor's horse.

By the time he returned, the twins and all the other young people were listening to the adults. "That Bettyjohn or Prettybroom or whatever that plantation colonel calls himself is crazy for trying to get his property back after all this time. Gilly should take those signs down. Besides, Lexington is too far west of Ashtabula. If those slaves had any sense, they'd have headed straight north for Toledo or Detroit," Father said.

"Clayton," said Louis Hathaway, "Gilly won't give up until those huge rewards are claimed."

And before Father could reply, Abel Quimby said, "Louis is right, Clayton. Biggest catch ever heard of in these parts. Why, even I'm keeping my ears and eyes open—I'd sure like to have that reward." All the men laughed, and some of the women smiled. "The Painesville *Telegraph* has had a daily story about the Pettybone runaways—"

Brian Owen-Smith interrupted him, "And the Cleveland papers are full up with stories—pictures, too."

"It's the money," Phoebee Pennypacker said, twisting her spider-thin fingers together. "Doctor Simmons, what do you think about all this ruckus?"

"Ruckus?" the doctor asked politely. "Just what do you mean?"

"I mean such wonderful rewards for these slaves. Why are they so all-fired important to their colonel, and why all this business about kidnapping and being held —AGAINST THEIR WILL—and that kind of nonsense."

"It isn't nonsense, Phoebee," the doctor said quietly. "You know, I've been a guest at MarbleHall."

There was a gasp from the group, but the doctor just smiled.

"And you know from the newspapers that these slaves are the very first ever to escape from MarbleHall. You wouldn't have any way of knowing this, but everywhere in the South, MarbleHall has a reputation for treating its slaves unusually well. In fact, they get such benevolent treatment that a Southerner would call it freedom. Now what slave would want to escape from a paradise like that, Phoebee?" He paused, letting his words sink in. "The crux of the matter is this: the myth of the Pettybone paradise is gone, and the luster of the Pettybone name is tarnished. And that's why the Pettybones claim their slaves were kidnapped—to save face. To a Southerner, the loss of the respectability of his honored name is the worst of all humiliations."

"So it's not their pocketbook that's pinching," Phoebee said. "It's their precious reputation that's hurting."

"I couldn't have said it better myself." The doctor bowed to her. Phoebee preened herself at the doctor's praise.

"If I were going after those kidnapped runaways, I'd surely do it differently," scoffed Daniel.

"And how would that be?" Doctor Simmons asked pleasantly.

"I'd—"

Father interrupted Daniel, saying, "Doctor, why don't we men go down to the south pasture. I've got a matched pair down there I'm mighty happy about." He got up and all the men followed, strolling around the house and out of sight. Lloyd Owen-Smith hurried after them, for that left him the only grown boy amid eight girls.

"Well, ladies." Momma got up. "Shall we begin getting the food together?" She waved away the girls, who came forward to help. "You all have a holiday since it's a birthday party."

As the women went in, Victory heard Susan Quimby ask, "Are you feeling well, Sarah? Your face is all flushed."

"Fit as a fiddle, Susan. It's just so warm. . . ." The rest of her answer was lost in the chatter of the women.

"Victory, let's show them Nugget," Faith said, and the girls all ran to the pasture near the stables where the mares and foals were grazing.

"I'm scared of horses," Margaret Hathaway said as Victory climbed the gate and motioned the other girls over.

"Bring Nugget here, Victory," Faith said. Victory crooned to Golden Dawn, and the mare lifted her head and came trotting toward her mistress. Nugget kicked up her tiny heels and galloped after her. Victory brought them close, and each of the girls put a hand through the gate to pet the horses. Nugget turned away and chased a butterfly. "Show them how you can ride, Victory," Faith urged. Victory stepped from the gate onto Golden Dawn's back and kicked her gently with her heels. They went off at a quick trot about the pasture, skirts flying, pantaloons showing. Just then Momma rang the bell from the house calling everyone in to eat. The girls all raced to the pump to wash, then went into the dining room.

Faith sat between Doctor Simmons and Louise. Victory sat opposite her between Mary Hathaway and Homer. The other guests spread out down both sides of the long table, which was so laden with food that the tablecloth didn't show anywhere. After the silent grace, everyone began to eat. They ate and ate and ate. At last Father pushed his chair back on its hind legs and put his hands across his stomach. "Sarah, that was a meal fit for a king."

A flurry of compliments on Momma's cooking continued as the women got up and cleared the platters and dishes from the table. A stack of small plates was set before both Victory and Faith and a large knife by each stack. A hush fell, then the kitchen door opened and Momma appeared, Susan Quimby just behind, each carrying a large cake sprouting thirteen small lighted candles.

"Happy birthday. . . ." Father started. Everyone sang, then the twins sliced their cakes while Momma poured more strong hot coffee and Susan Quimby filled the children's milk glasses. The cakes vanished and conversation lagged, everyone too full to talk.

"You men and young folks scoot," Momma waved her hands, "and leave the kitchen to us ladies."

"Let's play drop the handkerchief," Faith cried. Everyone joined in, and soon they were all laughing and sweaty. Tiring of the game, they trouped back to the horse pasture. "Ride bareback for us again, Victory," Mary Hathaway pleaded. Victory didn't need a second invitation and did her performance again. Faith, not to be outdone, ran to the barn and brought Redgirl, who had been penned up with the other dogs. "Victory had a foal, but I'm going to have puppies," she announced grandly.

"Oh, when . . . ?"

"Can I have one . . . ?"

"What are you going to name them . . . ?"

Faith didn't answer or promise, but she'd stolen the stage from Victory.

The afternoon sun was low in the sky when the guests left. All the Strawbridges stood in the barnyard and waved to each family as it drove out the lane. Homer hugged Victory. "That was some party," he said happily. "You've entered your teens." Victory hugged him back, but over his shoulder she saw Momma scratching, her face red and feverish.

"I'm going up to lie down, Clayton."

Father looked after her and shook his head. "She refused to let me say a thing to Doctor Simmons while he was here because she said it would just add to his evidence."

"But, Father, she looked awfully red today—Mrs. Quimby asked her if she were feeling all right, and Momma smoothed cornstarch on her face before dinner. Didn't you notice?"

"No." Father pulled his beard. "But I reckon that Simmons did. Tell me again—did Clarasue say that rash was just southern?"

"Yes, just southern—for sure. First the rash and fever, then all of a sudden the rash begins to ooze and the cough comes. It all goes away by itself after a month or more."

"Month or more?" Father looked stern. "That's a mighty long time to itch and ooze and cough."

"Too long," Victory said. "Father, Doctor Simmons hasn't done anything about the doll-charm. Can't we trust him, for Momma's sake?"

The question hung in the air unanswered.

Chapter 18

Ashtabula was in a tizzy!

Four days after the birthday party, the Painesville *Telegraph* trumpeted a banner headline:

PETTYBONE SLAVES HERE

Yesterday, Bull Boom, overseer of MarbleHall, almost captured the kidnapped Pettybone slaves who were in Douglass Heaton's boat leaving Mentor Harbor. Overseer Boom gave chase in Captain Morgan's cutter, but a sudden storm forced the Captain to put in at Fairport Harbor. The Heaton boat is unaccounted for.

Fairport Harbor's Constable Nutter, and Painesville's Constable Conklin, were told at once of the escaping runaways by Overseer Boom. A search would have been organized on the spot except for the ferociousness and length of the storm. Every male over sixteen has been ordered to join an official search party. All boat owners have been ordered onto the lake to search. As we go to press, no wreckage of the Heaton boat has been found or any of its occupants' bodies. Overseer Boom has southern bloodhounds with him, so it is unlikely that the fugitives can possibly escape by land; if, by some miracle, the Heaton boat didn't sink.

Victory and Homer had the paper spread before them on the kitchen table. "What do you think happened, Homer?" Victory asked. "Did they drown, or was the Good Lord with them?"

"Wish Father had let me go to Geneva with him today," Homer said. "I'd like to hear what's being said."

"But there's so much to do on the farm that he didn't want to take time to go himself," Victory said. "And it's just as bad inside. With Momma coming down so sick after the party, Faith and I are busier than two weasels in a hen house."

"How is she?" Homer asked.

"When Momma stays home from Meeting as she did last First Day, you know she's sick. Everything's happening just like Clarasue said it would."

"She ought to let Father call Doctor Simmons."

"Well, she won't."

"Got to go, sis. King's gone today, so I'm managing the crew clearing the north field. Bring lots of food when you come."

"It'll be Faith today. You know how she is about nursing."

"Wonder if Doctor Simmons is at his telescope searching the lake today?" Faith said, coming in from the yard, her apron full of eggs. Redgirl, her sides getting fatter every day, sat down on the doorsill.

"He should be here doctoring Momma," Victory said.

"She was pretending not to be sick because of our party, but now that it's over. . . ." Faith put the eggs away, then the girls washed their hands at the pump and began to make lunch for the men.

When they were finished, Faith snatched up the heavy basket and water jug, saying too eagerly, "I'll take it this time, Victory," and was out the door calling to Redgirl to come with her. Victory half smiled.

Picking up a carrot, Victory ran to the pasture and crooned for Golden Dawn. She took a quick bareback ride, then slid off and returned to the house. Stoking the range, she put on water to boil for the washing. She'd have to wash Momma's things separately—that's what Momma did when one of them was sick.

The tray for Momma was ready, and Victory took it up to the bright sick room. Momma turned her head, opened her mouth to say something, but broke into a spasm of coughing. Victory set the tray down, got a glass of water, and held it to Momma's lips. She only gagged on it, so Victory set it down, got her out of the wet bed, sponged the draining rash, smoothed on the salve from the medicine box, put a clean dry nightgown over her head, and sat her in a chair with the lunch tray in her lap while she remade the bed with dry linen. "How's the lunch?" Victory asked, determined to be cheerful.

"Fine, but I think I'll just climb into bed again. I feel so tired." She did, and Victory pulled the blinds and opened two windows. As she took the tray down, she saw that Momma hadn't touched a thing on it. When she came back up to get the soiled laundry, Momma was asleep.

Victory hated wash day, and today was worse than ever, for she had two separate batches to do. Beginning with Momma's things she boiled everything in the copper boiler. Then she lugged the heavy washtubs into the back yard, set them up on boxes, poured hot water into one and cold into the remaining two tubs. Getting out the scrub board, she lifted the sheets from the copper boiler with a stick and carried them out to the tub of hot water. Up and down, up and down. She rubbed them with a cake of harsh laundry soap that made her hands smart like fire. The sun was hot, and perspiration ran down her face and neck. Straining, she lifted a sheet, heavy with water, wrung it out, dipped it into one tub of rinse water, wrung it again, and dropped it into the final rinse tub. Now she lifted it, squeezed it as dry as she could, then hung it on the clothesline. She began the second sheet. . . . By the time she was finished with just Mother's things, her shoulders were aching. Irritably she looked for Faith. She'd been gone long enough to take lunches to six different crews instead of one. Victory looked longingly toward the foal pasture, but instead went up to check on Momma. She was leaning over the side of the bed coughing up bloody sputum. Victory rushed to her, wiped her face and mouth with her wet apron, and eased her back onto her pillow. Momma lay back, exhausted. Victory put a hand on her forehead. It was hot and wet. She felt the bedclothes that she had just changed an hour ago. They were clammy. Patiently, Victory changed everything again, left Momma dry, and went downstairs with a new armful of special laundry to boil, scrub, and hang.

Victory was rubbing out the last of her brothers' socks

when Faith and Redgirl came around the shed and into the back yard. "Where on earth have you been?" Victory yelled. Faith flipped her head and didn't answer. "Well, smarty, you can just finish up the wash and take down the dry laundry and put it all away and clean up everything—and get supper besides, 'cause you haven't helped one bit. And what's more, Momma's getting sicker by the minute, and I'm going to have to sit with her." She left without another word and ran up to Momma. She was awake and scratching.

"You mustn't scratch, Momma, it's—"

"Can't help it, Victory—the itching's. . . ."

"Shall I tie your hands to the bedpost?" Momma grimaced, but Victory ran out to get some strong cord. Before she tied Momma, she changed all the wet things for clean dry ones once again. Carefully she wound the cord about Momma's wrists and ankles and tied each loosely to the bedpost, for with her coughing fits she needed leeway to lean over to the chamber pot that Victory had pulled from under the bed.

"Read to me, Victory?" Momma asked. "The Psalms." Victory took the Bible from the mantel and read all of Momma's favorites, then began at the beginning and was on Psalm 29 when it got so dark she had to light a candle. The sound of a galloping horse coming up the lane stopped her reading. "Is that Clayton?" Momma reared up only to fall back, held by the cords. "Go ask him to come to me right away." She looked eagerly toward the door. Victory went down the stairs and outside. Father had dismounted, and Faith and Redgirl were beside him with a lantern. Victory ran toward him, then slowed when she saw the expression on his face. It was as if he were bursting with a hundred secrets to tell.

"Get supper on the table, twins, quick. I'm going to round up the boys. I got more news than a dog has fleas." And before Victory could open her mouth, he jogged off toward the stable, pulling Gretchen Girl behind him.

Victory went back up to Momma and explained Father's news. But Momma waved it away, saying, "Tell him to hurry, Victory."

Chapter 19

"Father, Momma wants to see you right away," Victory said as he came in. "She's gotten an awful lot worse today, and she's asking for you." They went up to the sick room.

"Tied!" Father exclaimed. "Sarah, what's the meaning of this?" He knelt beside her and put his big cool hand on her hot cheek.

"Clayton, I couldn't spoil the twin's party, so I've been holding back, but now the itching. . . . Victory tied me so I couldn't scratch."

"I'm getting Doctor Simmons." Father rose.

"No." Momma stopped him. "Not tonight. If I'm not better tomorrow, maybe then."

"You sure, Sarah?"

"Yes. Now that you're home, I'll rest easy. You two go down and have your supper, and I'll hear all about Geneva later. And, Victory, don't bother about supper for me." Victory left the candle on the table beside the bed, and she and Father left, reluctantly.

Once in the lantern-bright kitchen, Father sat down, the family about him. Faith had supper on the table, but the food cooled as Father told his tale.

"Geneva's a rumor mill," he said. "The Pettybone slaves have been reported sighted in twenty different places. Constable Luke in Geneva has guards posted at the dock and railroad station. No one's tending to business. It's as if war had been declared, and all the men had gone off, leaving behind only females, young'uns, and misfits. Riding home, I saw a farmer's wagon searched by a gang of men. Tore all the bags of grain open and then got down under the wagon to be sure there weren't any secret compartments. Finally let the farmer go.

"People I talked to said that Overseer Boom has split the search parties, and he's with the one that's coming our way. He could be here tomorrow."

"Right here—in plain little old Ashtabula—tomorrow?" Faith asked.

"I talked to Deputy Weed just before I rode home. Gilly's search party was just coming back when I was riding down Main Street. Rode up close to Weed, 'cause he doesn't have sense enough to keep his mouth shut. He said that they'd searched along the lake front, in and out of those caves in the cliffs, halfway down to Geneva. He told me he thinks Gilly's crazy to think he'll find the slaves this far from Mentor. But what he told me that bothered me the most was that Gilly's most likely going to order all males to join an official search party tomorrow or the next day, depending if they find Heaton's boat or some bodies."

"Will we go?" Peter asked.

"No," Father said. "Now, not a word of this to your mother. I'm getting Doctor Simmons tomorrow if she

111

isn't better. Now eat up. I want everyone to get a good night's sleep. We'll all need our wits sharp as thorns for the next forty-eight hours."

The next day began like any other except that none of Father's hired hands showed up. "Off slave-hunting on their own," Father said disgustedly. The *Telegraph* reported that Overseer Boom and the Geneva constable had organized an official search party that was coming ever eastward. Neither party, east nor west, had found anything yet.

Father and his sons exercised the horses and worked in the fields all morning. Victory washed. Faith helped —strung the clothesline, put the washtubs on boxes in the yards and filled them with water, and put the copper boiler on the stove, but once Victory came down with her arms filled with a second batch of dirty linen from the sick room, she said, "I'm going over to Lilac's. I have to tell her something—important."

"You stay here and help," Victory said crossly. "I want some time today with Nugget. Homer said he'd help me begin to halter break her."

"I'll only stay a minute, Victory. Please? It's awfully important."

Victory gave up. "Oh, go on then."

"I'll make it up to you, don't worry, and I'll only be a minute," Faith said already out the door and racing across the barnyard, Redgirl beside her.

Victory did the washing, then checked on Momma. She was moaning and twisting back and forth, rubbing her itching back against the soaked sheet. Victory tried to get her to drink something, but Momma just went on with her frantic rolling.

When the men came in for lunch, Father and Victory went right up. Father took one look at Momma and said quietly, "I'm riding for that doctor." He went out, and Victory started to change Momma's soaked bed again. She picked up the pile of soggy laundry and was about to leave the room when she heard Father on Gretchen Girl gallop down the lane. She turned to the window and saw Father slow and stop at the clump of trees at the end of the lane. He dismounted, and leading Gretchen Girl, disappeared into the trees. Victory felt breathless. She'd seen him go into those trees once before. What could be in there that was so important that it would make him stop when he was hurrying to the doctor? Father and Gretchen Girl reappeared, and Father mounted and was soon out of sight. Victory went down to the kitchen. The boys had finished lunch and gone, but Faith's plate was untouched.

" 'Only a minute.' Drat you, Faith. You're not being fair," Victory yelled at the range as she began to lug water in to boil. Sighing, she cleaned up the dishes, then returned to the washing. She was up to her elbows in suds when she heard hoofbeats. Father had found the doctor. Victory smiled for the first time that day. Served Faith right to miss the doctor, by taking advantage of her 'only a minute.' She caught the bridles of the horses as they came to a halt in the barnyard. "Welcome, Doctor Simmons," she said.

"I swear you're prettier now than you were when you were twelve," the doctor said as he undid his black bag from the saddle. Homer came limping from the stables and took the two horses. "How's that leg, Homer?"

"Fine. Never did thank you for what you did for me." Homer held out his hand to the doctor, and they shook, hard.

"Glad I could help." The doctor dismissed Homer's thanks. "Don't favor that leg—use it—and that limp'll be gone in a few months." Then he went to the pump, washed, and Father led the way to Momma's room, Victory trailing behind. He started when he saw the cords on Momma's wrists and ankles. "What's this?" he asked, stripping off his coat and going directly to Momma. "Cut those, Victory, so I can examine her." Victory got the scissors from the sewing basket and cut her loose. The doctor opened her sopping high-necked night-gown and started as he saw the oozing brown rash. "Get some boiling water, Victory."

She rushed to the kitchen and grabbed up the ever-warming teakettle on the stove. When she returned, the doctor had his stethoscope on her back. Father stood at the foot of the bed, following every move. "She didn't eat or drink anything at your party the other day," the doctor said. "How long's she had this?"

"I'm not sure," Father said. "Started out small—just an itchy patch on her back so she treated herself at first. Then when she got worse Clarasue came and said it was a bad fever, but that it would go away in time. But since the party, it's gotten much worse."

"Did Clarasue say what kind of fever this is?"

"No." Victory lied for Father.

"It's jumbo fever. I saw lots of it in Baltimore. You don't die from it but you suffer like hades." He drew the sheet up over Momma and took a vial of medicine from his bag. "Five drops of this in a small glass of water

114

three times a day. And, Clayton, if one of your sons will ride into town with me, I'll give him a salve that should ease the itching. And some other medicines, too. She's dehydrated. Why on earth didn't you call me sooner?"

"She's proud, Doctor. Wanted to cure herself, I guess."

"Get liquids into her, even if you have to force them down her, that's the most important thing now. We know she won't take any of my usual relaxing remedy." The doctor smiled at Father as he packed his bag.

"Have a cup of coffee with us, Doctor?" Father invited.

"That would taste mighty good, Clayton, but only while I wait for one of your sons to saddle up."

Father went to the door and let out a shout for Homer. "Saddle up, son, you're going into town with the doctor. And bring the doctor's horse."

Victory stood over the warming coffeepot. "Wonder how the slave hunting went today?" the doctor said.

"What hunting?" Father asked.

"Gilly and Weed and a bunch of men rode off toward Geneva about eight this morning. You think the slaves survived that storm, Clayton?"

"Don't see how they could have." Father shook his head.

"But no wreckage or bodies have been found." The coffee finally was hot, and Victory gathered up her apron and took hold of the hot handle.

There were the quick, light, running steps of a small person in the barnyard, then Faith burst in shouting, "Father—Father, it's all arranged. RIVER STRAIGHT, and you'll—" Victory let the coffeepot crash to the floor and jumped to avoid the scalding liquid. Faith stopped long enough to turn about. Then, and only then, did she see Doctor Simmons.

"Clumsy of me," Victory said. "But you scared me out of my wits exploding in here like a Fourth of July bomb."

"I'm sorry, Victory." Faith knelt to pick up the pot while Victory got several rags to wipe up the floor.

"So what's all arranged, Faith, and who's River Straight?" the doctor asked.

"A horse." Faith stood up and looked boldly at the doctor. "Father and a man in Jefferson have been dickering about our stallion, River Straight, and today I was over at Lilac's, and King said—"

"Don't bother the good doctor with that." Father laughed. "Faith, Victory, go tend your mother."

From their parents' room Victory and Faith saw the doctor and Homer ride down the lane a few minutes later. Victory's insides let go. She poured a glass of water, put the medicine into it, tipped Momma's head, and held the glass to her lips. It took a long time, but finally the glass was empty.

Faith sat dumbly in the rocking chair. Victory started to change the bed. Had the dropped coffeepot saved them, or did the doctor now know for certain that there were immediate plans afoot? First the doll-charm, then Momma's jumbo fever, and now "it's all arranged" and "RIVER STRAIGHT." Yet without the doctor, Homer would be dead. Victory went on cleaning and drying Momma and tried to blot out the scene in the kitchen.

Chapter 20

Father came in very quietly as Victory finished. He looked at Momma, saw that her eyes were closed, then motioned the twins to come with him. Victory dropped the pile of laundry, and they all went down to the kitchen. Daniel, Paul, and Peter were all there at the oval table.

Father motioned Faith and Victory to be seated, then drew up another chair, its back toward Faith. He straddled it with his big legs and asked in measured tones. "Now just what, daughter, is 'all arranged' for me about RIVER STRAIGHT?"

Faith looked at him, and her answer came as boldly as she'd lied to the doctor. "Keeping the Pettybone slaves. They're being brought to the river entrance tonight."

A silence descended on the kitchen. Father didn't even raise his hand to stroke his beard. He just looked into Faith's eyes.

"Go on," Father said. Now his hand did move to his beard, and the worry wrinkles came.

"I went over to Lilac's today 'cause I had something

important to tell her, but she had to see Cozetta Cratty about something, so I went along," Faith said. "Cozetta was alone 'cause her dad, Crazy Cratty, and her brothers, Tuck, Little Leroy, and Uranus, had all gone fishing down Mentor way and hadn't come home since the storm. But that hadn't bothered Cozetta any 'cause they often stay out three, four days and nights at a stretch. She hadn't seen the paper—"

"Just the essentials," Father snapped.

"Well," Faith swallowed, "while Lilac and Cozetta were talking, Tuck came loafing up the path. He whispered in Cozetta's ear, then Cozetta whispered in Lilac's ear."

"Did anyone whisper in your ear?" Father asked, his tone even again.

"Not till we got back to Clarasue's. Lilac commenced whispering in her momma's ear, and by that time I was so riled up I started to walk home, but Clarasue stopped me. She let out a big halloo, and King came running in from the barn. 'It's them Pettybones,' Clarasue said. 'Crazy Cratty came on that Heaton boat turned bottomside up. But no one was hanging on to it. Tuck's daddy sailed around some and found four of the runaways bobbing like corks in life jackets, but he couldn't find the other two. He looked for them till it got too dark to see, but finally he gave up. He rode out the storm in a cove near Fairport Harbor. Then, when the waves let up, he sailed up the shore and into the harbor here before daybreak.

" 'He's got the four slaves hid in his boat, but he wants them off, quick. So he sent Tuck to tell Cozetta to get a message to Mr. Strawbridge. The cave's the

118

only safe place for them now. So, it's RIVER STRAIGHT *tonight.*' King just nodded. Then they all looked at me and told me to come home fast as I could and tell you to get the cave open and things ready."

Faith stopped speaking. Father nodded as if confirming something, his worry wrinkles deep. "Daughters, get the hampers ready, and Peter, take them down the Liberty Well as fast as you can. I'm going to unleash Blueboy until supper. He'll let us know if there are any snoopers about. We're in the gravest danger we've ever been in since this station started operating."

"But what are you so afraid of, Father?" Daniel asked.

"Informers—Gilly, Weed, Doctor Simmons. For this kind of money I wouldn't trust my best friend to keep his mouth shut about me—us—the station. The minute that boat or those bodies are found, the search will focus on the area around them—" He broke off. "But we've got to act natural, so boys, the chores. Come."

Victory was already getting the hampers out. The twins filled them full of sandwiches, fruit, cold chicken and ham and filled two extra water jugs. Peter came in just as they had finished. As he was stuffing the containers into the big sack, he said, "Father and the Good Lord sure have their hands full this time, don't they?" He shouldered the sack and went out whistling. "Hurry with supper, I'm starving. Hey, here's Homer."

Homer gave the salve and other medicines to the twins, and they told him what had happened while he had been saddling the horses. "The doctor didn't say anything suspicious on the ride. We talked medicine mostly." He went out to find Father.

Victory poured some grape juice into a pitcher, took

the medicines and put them in a small bag, then went up to Momma while Faith began supper. Momma took half a glass of juice, then Victory changed her bed, wiped her clean, rubbed on the doctor's salve, and put a clean gown on her. When she slipped out, she left the door open.

Supper was hurried and silent until Paul growled, "RIVER STRAIGHT. So Doctor Simmons even knows the password. Sitting ducks—all because of our 'safe' cave. Some friends we've got, leaving us to juggle the hottest potatoes ever to come over the Railroad. What plans are there for moving them on?"

"Don't know yet," Father said.

"The cave *is* the safest place for them now," Peter said, "and the trail from the boat up to the cave entrance is such a short one that it'll be a miracle if those bloodhounds find it."

Father got up. "RIVER STRAIGHT is sure to be right after dark. Daniel, to the river entrance; Paul, guard the shed; Peter, get Blueboy and go to the front. I'm going down to the river." They all went out.

The twins began to clear away the dishes. Faith dropped a meat platter, and it broke into thirteen pieces. She just stood looking down at the mess as if it weren't real.

"Victory—I'm scared."

Chapter 21

Faith cried herself to sleep.

Victory, too anxious to sleep, got up, lighted a candle, and went to her parents' room. She went through the ritual of cleaning and drying the rash, smoothing on the new salve, getting Momma into a dry nightgown, and then back into the changed bed. She held a glass of juice to her lips. Momma took all of it in slow sips. "Where's Clayton, Victory?"

"He'll be up a little later," Victory said.

"Stay with me until he comes."

"Of course, Momma." Victory set the candle on the stand by the bed and sat down in the rocking chair. The clock chimed away two hours. It began to rain. Getting up, she went to the window. As she returned to the rocker, she saw Father standing in the doorway.

"How is she, daughter?" he whispered.

"About the same. Are they here, Father?"

"No, they didn't come. We waited two extra hours, then gave up. I sent Paul and Peter to bed. Daniel and I'll watch." His voice was weary and very troubled. "Will you stay with Momma, daughter. I'll be on the back porch with Blueboy if you need me."

The room was warm, and Victory opened two windows in spite of the rain. Putting a light blanket on Momma she returned to the rocker.

Suddenly sharp sounds mingled with the steady downpour. Victory was out of the chair like a shot and crouching at the window, her ear to the opening. The sounds came again. She should have recognized them the first time, she chided herself as she darted into her room, threw a robe about her, and flew quickly down the front stairs. Unbolting the front door, she opened it wide and stepped out onto the porch calling softly, "ERIE SHORES—RIVER STRAIGHT."

Victory saw five figures rise from the shadow of the porch. They came silently up the steps and into the hall. The smell of fish came with them. A gravelly voice said, "Fetch dese mens ta yah pa." The man turned and was gone.

Victory closed the door and bolted it. That voice—it sounded like—no, it couldn't be. . . .

"Join hands and follow me," she said, for it was almost pitch black in the hallway. She felt a wet hand grasp hers, and she led the way into the kitchen where the dying fire in the range cast a slight glow.

Blueboy growled. "What do you hear, boy?" Father whispered as Victory pulled the kitchen door open.

"Father, RIVER STRAIGHT is here."

"Come." Father led the fugitives across the barnyard. Victory followed, unbidden. Father opened the shed door, and the four blacks slipped through, silent as shadows. Victory moved in behind and pulled the shed door closed as Father shot the bolts back and entered

122

the secret room. He lighted a candle and whispered, "Come." The fugitives hesitated, but Victory pushed on the last one. They were the Pettybone runaways without a doubt.

"Hurry," she said. "There's food and dry clothes and beds waiting for you down there."

Father opened the trapdoor, and one by one the slaves clambered down the iron rung ladder in the side of the well. Father lighted candles below, had the double locks of the door to the cave open, and guided the slaves down the narrow corridor, Victory on their heels. She lighted more candles. Nobody paid any attention to her. The dripping stinking runaways crowded about the hampers and water jugs, drinking and stuffing food into their mouths with both hands. Pity welled up in Victory for the missing one—it must have been a jockey, for before her stood two giants and two tiny men, even shorter than Peter. And that Heaton man? Was he dead or alive?

"Rest easy," Father said. "You're safer here than if you were in heaven. Eat and sleep." The slaves listened, but didn't answer, for they were gobbling food and draining the water jugs. The fearful expressions hadn't left their faces in spite of Father's words. "We'll bring you more food soon. Good night and sleep well." Father motioned Victory up the corridor before him. The slaves turned and called after them:

"God bless you, Underground peoples." Father locked the double locks on the door, and they were topside in two minutes, where they found Blueboy sitting at the entrance to the shed and the rain still pounding down.

"Victory, will you stay here with Blueboy while I

go tell Daniel they're here?"

"Yes."

Father drove his fist into the palm of his hand. "If I only knew . . . ?" He stopped abruptly. "Who brought them, Victory?"

"A gravelly-voiced man—a voice I've heard but. . . ."

"You've told me enough," Father interrupted and slipped out the door. He was back soon. "Now, Victory, one more task for you. Sit with your mother tonight. I'm depending on you."

Victory's shoulders stiffened proudly. She slipped out the door and, keeping to the shadows, reached the kitchen door and went in. The clock chimed four as she lighted the candle and looked down at Momma. She was sleeping, her face wet, but her sheets were only slightly damp. Victory sighed with relief. She blew out the candle, went to her room, and changed into dry clothes. Then she returned to Momma's room and sat down in the rocking chair.

Chapter 22

At dawn Faith came into Momma's room. "What're you doing in here, Victory? Is Momma worse?"

"No, but Father wanted me to stay up with her."

"RIVER STRAIGHT?" Faith's voice faltered.

"Here and safely below." Victory told her sister what had happened during the night.

"Then I *didn't* spoil it. They just came another way," Faith said.

"Right. All's well so far."

"Wonder what happened that changed the plans?"

"I reckon Father's wondering, too. He's been guarding with Blueboy in the shed since they came, so make lots of coffee first thing. I'll be down as soon as I tend to Momma."

Victory gave Momma her dose of green medicine, then a glass of juice. She had her dry and changed in no time. "Want some breakfast?" Victory asked. Momma shook her head and closed her eyes. Victory went down with her load of wet linens. The warm light of the lanterns, the aroma of sausages frying and of coffee perking made Victory very sleepy. She dropped the laundry in the far corner. "I'll get the things from the springhouse," Victory said. She had to keep moving to stay awake.

At breakfast Father explained to Peter and Paul what had happened. Paul glowered. "Let the Strawbridges do it; they've never had a failure—yet." He glared around the table. "If we get out of this one without the secret going up in smoke, I'm a ring-tailed baboon."

"We'll build a cage and charge admission to see you," Peter quipped.

"Cut it out." Paul half rose in his chair and looked threateningly across the table at his brother.

"Stop!" Father said it so quietly that everyone stopped chewing. "We've enough troubles without quarreling among ourselves. We'll all work together on these Pettybones or Paul may be. . . ." He left the sentence hanging. Victory finished it for him in her mind—"right."

"It's a normal farm day. Chores, delivering those horses to Ravenna—"

"But Father, nobody should leave now. We're all needed here," Daniel said.

"*I gave my word* that those horses would be delivered today, and they are going to be, regardless." Father got up. "Peter, get the hampers from the cave so the girls can fill them again. Daniel and Paul, get those Ravenna horses ready. No shipment is going to keep me from my business word." The boys got up and went out, and Father went upstairs to see Momma.

It was half an hour later that Faith and Victory heard a horse on the U drive. Father came bounding down the front stairs, unbolted the door, then slammed it shut

126

and rebolted it. He came striding into the kitchen. "Get the boys," he ordered.

The sheet of paper was lying on the kitchen table when the twins' brothers trooped in, followed by the girls. They all gathered around Father. The paper that lay on the table had been poorly printed, but the message was clear. Gilly was organizing an official search party. All males over sixteen were to report—with horse, hounds, and guns if they possessed any of these—to Constable Gilly's office by nine o'clock at the latest—*today*. The purpose: to look for the four remaining Pettybone slaves. One drowned body of a jockey had been found on the beach only two miles west of Ashtabula. Overseer Boom was in town with his bloodhounds and clothing with the runaways' scents on them. Any person defying this order would be arrested.

"We going, Father?" Daniel asked.

"No." Father tossed the notice into the range's firebox. "Twins, the hampers done?"

"Yes, Father. Peter took them down before the notice came."

"Daniel and Paul, are the Ravenna horses ready?"

"Yes," Daniel said, then burst out. "Father, don't send us. Anything could happen today, and we may be needed—"

"You and Paul get started right now," Father ordered calmly. Everyone went outside. Twenty-five horses were tied in two lines. Paul and Daniel mounted. "My regards to Cousin John and Anna, and thank them for putting you up. Don't tell them about your mother's illness. We'll expect you Second Day before sundown," Father called after them as they started out the lane.

127

The girls went back into the house. The clock chimed six.

"I'd better go check on Momma," Victory said and went upstairs. Momma was asleep. Victory felt very, very sleepy, and she sat down in the rocker for just a minute.

The barks from the dogs and horsemen on the U drive woke her. Bolting from the room, she ran down the back stairs and onto the back porch. Faith stood there, her hands to her face. The dogs' barking had brought Homer from the shed and Peter from the near pasture where he had been exercising some of the horses. As the men rode into the barnyard, they encircled Homer and Peter. Just then Father came running from behind the barn. He halted when he saw the patrol, for every man had a rifle across his saddle. Father quieted the dogs with a word.

"Clayton?" It was Hugh Hanson. "Where're the rest of your boys?" Victory watched Father's face. She saw rage give way to resignation.

"Paul and Daniel have gone to deliver twenty-five horses to a buyer in Ravenna."

"That'd better be the truth, Clayton," Mr. Hanson said, "'cause if it ain't, you'll be in bigger trouble than you're in already."

"You know my word, Hugh. What're you doing in my barnyard with guns?"

"You and your boys here is under arrest for not showing up for Constable Gilly's search party." Three of the men dismounted, took down their rifles, and waved Father, Homer, and Peter into the stables. Victory and Faith stood, watching everything. Father and their brothers came from the stable, mounted, each closely guarded. Then Hugh Hanson said, "Bill, Sam, you stay here. If anything like carriages or boats on the river or anyone tries to talk to these young'uns or their momma, arrest whoever and whatever it is and hold it here. Understand?" Sam and Bill nodded. The patrol herded the three Strawbridge men into their midst and rode off toward town. Victory and Faith watched, too stunned to move.

"Just you two here?" Sam asked, slipping his rifle into the holster on his saddle and coming up to them.

"Momma's upstairs in bed—sick," Victory said.

"Two silly girls and a sick woman." Sam turned away and walked toward Bill who was tending their horses at the fence by the lane. "A plague on that Hugh Hanson anyway. I was a'hankerin' for some ridin' and excitement today, and what do I get?" He glared at the girls. "Don't even have a bottle to help while the day away."

"I brung some." Bill took a bottle from his saddlebag and shook it. "It's most empty, but it's better than nothin'." He took a swig, then passed it to Sam. Sam finished it and tossed it over his shoulder. He swore. Then both men walked to the shade of the apple tree and sat down. Redgirl and White had rushed off after a rabbit, but Blueboy stood at the end of his taut chain and growled at the two guards. They ignored him, and finally he gave up and settled back in his doghouse.

The twins went in and shut the kitchen door. Faith began tapping the floor with her toe and looking wise. Victory caught her meaning at once.

Below where the guards sat were the very prizes that

the patrol was looking for.

The twins began to giggle. It was so ridiculous, so impossible. They ran into the parlor and grabbed up cushions to smother their hysterical laughter. They laughed until they cried, wiping their faces with the pillows. They fell onto the couch, exhausted.

"So, it's you, me, Momma, those guards, and the shipment," Victory said. All their laughter drained away as their imprisonment and responsibilities became real to them.

Victory went up to see if Momma had heard all the commotion, but she was dozing. When she got back to the kitchen, Faith was dancing a jig and giggling again. She took Victory's shoulders, shook them, and one word burst from her lips.

Chapter 23

"WHISKEY!"

Victory looked at her twin, and in a second they were dancing a double jig. "Faith, you're a genius. Those bottles are out in the garden at the end of the second bean row, and if Sam and Bill see me, I'll be picking beans." Victory grabbed a big spoon and slipped out the dining room door. The three bottles were deeper than she had remembered, but finally she had them un-covered and lying on the ground beside her. Picking enough beans to hide the bottles, she gathered up her apron and crept back to the house.

Faith was fixing lunch for the guards. "We'll wine and dine our guests as proper Quakers should," she said innocently. Victory went out to the springhouse to get cream, butter, eggs, and some other food.

"Where you think you're goin', girlie?"

"To the springhouse. My sister and I are making you some lunch," Victory said.

"Go on then." Sam waved her away. Victory got what she needed and smiled at the men as she returned, her apron loaded.

The lunch was: Momma's special spicy sausage (to

make the guards thirsty), mashed potatoes and salty gravy, buttered parsnips, biscuits, butter and strawberry jam, apples, a custard pie, and half a spice cake. They arranged the food on two trays and used the third tray for the glasses and just two bottles of whiskey. They'd keep one in reserve, just in case. They carried the trays out to the two men and put them down on the grass before them. Redgirl and White came sniffing, but Faith took them and shut them up in the barn. "Hope you like it?" Victory said.

"Thank you, miss, thank you indeed." Sam raised his cap to her. Victory dropped him a curtsey and turned back toward the house. Faith came in the dining room door from the barn, and they peeked at the two guards. Both men had the caps off their bottles and were drinking, heads tilted far back.

"Thank you, God, for Doctor Simmons and his remedies," Faith said, as the noise in the yard became more and more boisterous. The girls waited and watched. Finally it was quiet outside. The twins tiptoed onto the back porch.

The two bottles were empty, the food on the trays half eaten, and Bill and Sam were snoring. The twins picked up the trays and bottles and went back to the house and locked the kitchen door. Once inside they opened the window that looked out over the side porch to let air into the hot kitchen. They began to clear up the trays. "How long does a man stay drunk?" Faith asked.

"Dey'll stay drunk rest a da afternoon," said a low gravelly voice from behind them.

Victory whirled. *That voice!* Faith turned slowly. There, framed in the open window, stood Skinhead.

132

Chapter 24

"Don't be a'feard. I's comed ta help, 'n I ain't got no time ta waste. Furst—two tings. Yur pa 'n brudders, dey be in jail, but not hurts. Second ting, yah gots dem slaves down de well dat I brung last night?"

It was you, Victory wanted to shout, but instead said calmly, "Yes, they're here."

"Good." Skinhead crawled through the open window, gun in hand. Seeing that Humpty Dumpty body come over the sill turned Victory's legs to jelly.

"Coffee?" Faith backed toward the range.

"No time," Skinhead said, putting his rifle down on Momma's table. "Sits down 'n listen careful 'n *remember* what I tells yah. Now heres de plans. Faith, yah gets yurself dressed up like a boy 'n Victory, yah packs da food. Den Faith, yah leads dose runaways out de river exit 'n over ta Cratty's place. Cozetta'll lead dem from dere. Her pa's a'waitin' at Smuggler's Cove, 'n he'll take dem 'cross de lake soon as dey gets aboard. Yah come back here soon as yah gets de slaves ta Cozetta's—hear? Should only take yah a couple of hours ta do dat. Both yah gals gotta be home ifn dose guards should wake up or a search party come out here.

133

"Now, Victory, whiles Faith's doin' dat, yah keeps watch. Ifn someone or a search party should come, yah'll have ta use yur wits 'n hold dem off from searchin'. Nobody must search dis here farm—no matter what! But Faith'll be back by two or three o'clock at da very latest, so dere'll be two sets a wits a'workin' ifn dere's searchin' trouble. Now, yah gots all dat straight in yur heads?" he asked, leaning toward them.

The twins nodded. He tipped his greasy cap, picked up his gun, and went out the window without another word. They ran to the parlor and watched him go quickly down the lane into that special clump of trees on the pike, come out mounted on a horse, and gallop off toward town.

"Skinhead, of all people," Faith said as the girls flew back to the kitchen. "Can we trust him, Victory?"

"He brought the slaves last night," Victory said. "I remember his voice. He must be one of us, else he wouldn't know about the Liberty Well and the Pettybones."

"But still it could be a trick." Faith sounded doubtful.

"We'll have to take that chance," Victory replied, even though she found Skinhead's new role as unbelievable as Faith. "Not a minute to spare, Faith. Go get ready, and I'll make the food." Faith was back in about three minutes dressed in some of Peter's clothes, a cap hiding her braids. "Peter Strawbridge, how well you're looking today." Victory wagged her head and smiled at Faith's disguise. "Here's the food, now off with you, and God be with you."

Faith stepped onto the porch, looked at the sleeping guards, went straight to the shed, and disappeared. With

Faith gone, Victory's thoughts began to run wild.

Skinhead! What if Faith was right and he'd lied and they were delivering the Pettybone slaves into Bull Boom's hands instead of . . . ? Just then she heard Momma coughing. Victory dashed up to her. The spasm passed, then Momma said, "I'm hungry and thirsty."

For the second time that day, Victory could hardly believe her ears. She gave Momma a glass of water, then a second. "I'll bring up some bread and milk and make custard for later," she said. Victory went down to the kitchen, half her heart singing because Momma seemed better, but the other half in her shoes because she still wasn't sure she could believe in Skinhead. She returned with the tray of bread and milk and more juices. Putting the tray down, she got Momma clean and dry, then helped her to one of the chairs by the fireplace and put the tray on her lap. Momma ate while Victory changed the bed.

"My this tastes good, Victory." When she was done, Victory settled her in bed again. "Now will you read to me from the Bible?"

It was the last thing in the world Victory wanted to do, but she didn't want Momma to suspect anything. She got the Bible from the mantel, but Momma began coughing. Victory gave her the green medicine, and gradually the coughing stopped. Then Victory read from the Psalms until, in about fifteen minutes, Momma was dozing, and she could put the Bible down and tiptoe out.

She felt weak from sleeplessness, yet very nervous about all she had to do. Gathering cleaning things together, she scrubbed everywhere the Pettybone slaves had stepped on the porches and in the house. Then she and Blueboy walked all about the front yard, back and forth and around and around. Quietly she and Blueboy went into the back yard. The guards were still sleeping, so she and her dog repeated their parading about the barnyard. In the shed they did the same thing. She also took harness ointment and dropped it about on the floor. No fish smell remained after her work.

Before she went in, she chained Blueboy and put feedbags on Bill's and Sam's horses. Then back in the kitchen, she sank into a chair. Her insides felt as if a miniature lake storm had somehow gotten in and was blowing her thoughts and feelings in crazy circles. Getting up, she went back to Momma's room. She was scratching in her sleep, but Victory didn't stop to tie her.

While she was making the custard, the clock bonged twice. Faith should be back any minute now according to the plan. The custard was done, it was half-past two, and Victory looked toward the riverbank.

No Faith.

She'd be here in a minute. Victory sat down in Father's big arm chair to wait, and she was asleep before her head nodded twice.

Momma's call woke her. Groggily she looked about the kitchen. Then she remembered and leaped out of the chair. Leaning out the door, she was relieved to see that the guards still snored under the apple tree. So she ran up to Momma and found her coughing and oozing. She gave her one of the other medicines that the doctor had sent and that eased the cough. As she changed Momma, she asked. "Do you want the custard now?" Momma nodded no. Victory left her reading the Bible.

Once downstairs she made a frantic search for Faith. She was nowhere. What had happened? What should she do? It was nearly seven o'clock and no Faith—no Faith. Victory went out into the barnyard. The cows were standing at the gate, waiting to be milked. Victory glanced at the still-sleeping guards as she opened the gate, and the cows stampeded into their stalls. Redgirl and White ran out of the barn as Victory opened the door for the cows. She closed the stanchions, and the cows began to feed on the hay before them. While she milked them, all she could think of was Faith and the plan. Was she in jail with Father, Homer, and Peter? And were the Pettybone runaways with them? With shaking hands, she poured the pails of milk into smaller containers with tight lids and stored these in the springhouse. It was nearly dusk and she needed a lantern finally. She lit one and then left it in the barn until she could come back to let the cows out for the night. It was time to go back to the house to check again on Momma. She was sitting up against her pillows. "Water, Victory," she coughed.

Victory gave her two glasses, and Momma took a long time to drink each one. "I'll have that custard now, and a scrambled egg, and a glass of cold milk."

"Right this minute, Momma." Victory put false joy into her voice, but her worry over Faith's absence now obsessed her. She burned the first batch of eggs, spilled the milk as she poured it into the glass, but finally she got the simple supper together and took it up on a tray.

"I'll manage myself, daughter." Victory placed a pillow across Momma's lap and put the tray on it. Then she pulled the shades and lighted two candles.

137

"Call me when you're finished, Momma, and I'll come get these dishes. I've got some things to do." Victory went out.

She climbed the attic stairs. It was now quite dark. From the windows she looked to the south, then to the north. No Faith anywhere. A strange glow appeared in the north—what could it be? She waited, praying that she'd see Faith somewhere, but finally she returned to Momma's room. "I'll just read a little till I fall asleep," Momma said, gently scratching.

Victory was too agitated to stop to change Momma, so she put the Bible on the bed beside her, picked up the tray and said, "Good night, Momma. Call me if you need anything."

She went to the kitchen, dropped the tray on the table and lit a lantern. The cows had to be let out, but something made her go up to the attic again. She stared at the growing glow in the north, and this time she began to tremble.

Torches!

No official search party—or even a mob maybe—would still be out this time of night unless they knew where they were going and what they were looking for. Victory closed her eyes and prayed out loud. "Lord, Lord, let me hear Thy Inner Voice now—now—now!" When she opened her eyes, she could begin to see the mob coming far up the pike. Victory held herself very still, waiting for the Inner Voice. Waiting—waiting—waiting. Through the window she watched the mob slowly draw nearer and nearer. They were headed for the Strawbridge Place, but something would not let her move from the tiny crescent-shaped window.

Then something released her. Down the winding attic stairs she went to the back porch. Blueboy was howling, and Redgirl and White were barking. Sam and Bill, awakened by the dogs, were up and staggering toward their horses. They never saw Victory as she flew by them.

Dashing headlong into the open barn door, she picked up the lantern she had left there, set it in the corridor where there was no straw or debris on the floor, kicked it over, then turned and started toward the stanchions that still held the cows. But the lantern rolled, the chimney broke, and the open flame caught along the side of the stall area. Fire raced along the straw and smoke began to billow up. Terrified at the unexpected speed of the flames, Victory reached the first stanchion and tried to open it, but before she could release it, the smoke became so thick that she was forced to back off down the corridor, choking and coughing. Catching up her apron, she covered her mouth and nose and tried to go back to the cows, but it was no use. Blindly she stumbled toward the door, stepping into the pail, half full of milk, that she had planned to pour into the dishes for the barn cats. She grabbed it, rushed out of the barn, and filled her lungs with fresh air. When she could breathe again, she started screaming hysterically, "Momma, Momma, the cow kicked the lantern over and the barn's on fire!"

The mob—or search party—had just turned in the lane, and at Victory's screams it rolled toward her like a tidal wave. The cows were mooing and bawling, and Victory's heart broke. "Save the cows," she shrieked. "Save the cows!"

The mob was now all about her, and her voice was lost in the crackling of the fire, the yelling of the men, the snorting and rearing of their horses as they smelled the smoke, and the bays of the hounds. Victory stood, tears streaming down her face, clinging to the half-filled milk pail, sobbing, "Save the cows! Save the cows! Someone save the cows!"

A strong pair of arms went around her, carried her to the porch, and set her down. "You just stay out of the way, girl. Fires is men's work."

Chapter 25

The mob swirled about among the spread-out farm
buildings. Smoke poured out the open door and all the
seams in the barn, and the glowing light of the fire
paled the moon. Victory stood rooted to the porch, the
milk pail still clutched in her hand. A man grabbed the
pail from her, muttering, "Crazy kid," as he rushed
toward the barn.

Victory stood seeing, but not believing. Men with
hats or kerchiefs pressed over their noses and mouths
ducked toward the open barn door, but they fell back
as the smoke billowed out and the bellowing of the cat-
tle rose to a crescendo. A final death bawl soared into
the night. The reeking smell of charred flesh floated on
the smoke-filled air, and the mob grew silent, tempo-
rarily stilled by their failure.

But only for a moment. "Form lines from the two
pumps," one man called. "Get pails, buckets, anything
you can find." Victory ran to the washhouse and threw
the washtubs out the door. Then she flung six pails after
the washtubs. Men scrambled to pick them up, fill them
at the house and barn pumps, and pass them down the

lines of men that snaked across the barnyard to the barn. As the empty pails began to come back, the lines split into two; one for the filled buckets, one for the empty ones.

Victory ran into the kitchen, stopped, almost fainted. Faith was crawling in the side window.

"Where have you been?" Victory whispered wildly.

"Never mind. I'll go change and come out and pretend I've been up tending Momma." Faith raced silently up the stairs. Hardly knowing what she was doing, Victory gathered pans, even crocks—anything that would hold water—and took them out to the men around the house pump. Then, when there were no more pots or dishes, she stood on the back porch wringing her hands. Silently Faith joined her, dressed, looking bewildered, and the twins clung together, tears rimming their eyes.

"It's no use, girls, the barn's done," a stranger said. "Haymow's caught. Only thing we can do now is water down the other buildings and try to save them."

The lines shifted, and men boosted other men onto the roofs of the shed, the stables, the corncrib, the hen house, and all the other buildings about the barn. Others put up a ladder, and several men climbed to the roof of the house. Full pails were passed up to these men, and they dampened down the peaked roofs of these buildings. Some men threw buckets of water against the sides of the buildings to wet the walls down.

Other men had rushed to the stables to lead the horses out, but no horses were there, for it was warm enough to leave them in the pastures all night. Several men began pulling wagons, hayricks, harnesses, tools, carriages, the sleigh, and all the contents of the shed into the barnyard away from the barn. Others gathered up the rabbits and hens and cocks and tossed them into the washouse. The moon was paled by the blazing barn.

In the midst of this holocaust, Momma came staggering out onto the back porch. "What—where—Clayton —who—barn . . . ?"

Victory and Faith ran to her and caught her arms. She stood with them staring at the growing light of the burning barn, at the organized mob, and at the huge black man who leaned alone against the washhouse, holding several bloodhounds tightly at leash, and taking no part in the fire fighting. Constable Gilly stood near him. "Who's that with Gilly?" Momma pointed.

Victory and Faith nodded to each other. It couldn't be anyone but Overseer Bull Boom.

"Just one of the men who came to help put out the fire, Momma," Victory said, praying that Momma was too confused to realize what was happening.

"Get back," roared one man. "She'll be a'comin' down soon."

The interior of the barn now glowed devil's red, for the walls and roof had caught. Men scattered, the bloodhounds bayed, and Victory left Momma and zigzagged across the barnyard, unleashed Blueboy and tugged him to the porch, then knelt beside him and held him tight. Redgirl and White cowered by Faith's skirts. Every man astride the peaked roofs of the other buildings scooted as far away from the flaming barn as possible. Before anyone could say more, half the barn's roof fell in. Giant sparks, great burning timbers, and bales of half-burned straw whirled into the air like skyrockets. Some landed on the wet roofs of the other buildings, but the men were there and poured water over the flaming debris from the buckets they held in readiness. Other men threw water over the burning things that landed in the barnyard and on all the farm machinery and wagons and carriages.

Now the flames and smoke towered into the sky as more air got to the fire. Men held their hats to their faces to ward off the awesome heat. They stood watching the brilliant scene, moving only to keep the men astride the roof tops supplied with filled buckets and splashing the walls with more water. By the light of the flames, Victory could see the horses in the barn pasture huddled together in the farthest corner away from the fire.

Victory put Blueboy in the kitchen, then she went back and eased Momma from Faith's arm and led her back upstairs. Momma sank into one of the chairs and scratched. As quickly as she could, Victory changed the bed and got Momma washed and dried, smeared new salve on the rash, gave her the green medicine, and put her into bed. "Read to me, Victory." Victory again read from the Psalms, and again Momma was dozing and scratching within a few minutes, and Victory slipped from the room, leaving the candle burning. She returned to the back porch, Blueboy's chain in her hand and he at her feet. Faith still stood there watching the unbelievable sight before her. She looked at Victory as she came and stood beside her. Their glance seemed to tell each other all. Skinhead's voice—"Nobody must search dis here farm—no matter what."—seemed to be in both their ears again.

A rumble, then a noise like a bomb, signaled the collapse of the east and north walls. One fell straight over into the blazing interior; the other sank gradually to the ground like a grand lady making a curtsey to a queen. The fire blazed up anew, and the men on the roofs and the ground were busy again.

The extravaganza before them held the men in silent clumps. They seemed to have forgotten their original purpose for coming. The blaze, which could be seen for miles around, had brought half the county out to watch. Buggies and wagons clogged the pike and lane where their owners had abandoned them to come into the back yard for a closer look and to ask questions.

Now everyone was waiting for the last two walls and the other half of the roof to cave in. Victory wondered if hell were like this—flames so hot they were icicle clear.

The fire took its time. Victory put the dogs in the kitchen, then went up to Momma's room. She had fallen into an uneasy sleep and was scratching. Victory blew out the candle and hurried back to the porch. The two walls still stood. The huge crowd filled the grounds, many standing on the farm equipment to get a better view. Men hoisted small children about their necks, and women stood on tiptoe.

"Thar she goes!"

The south and west walls buckled, leaned, seemed to bow to each other, then fell on top of one another like two gladiators. Again the men on the roofs and the ground were busy, and the crowd scattered. But this was the last big scene everyone had been waiting for. The barn was now a giant mound of flaring red-hot rubble.

"Well, guess that's that, girls. How'd you say it started?" drawled a voice.

"One of the cows kicked the lantern over. I'm not very good at milking 'cause my brothers and father always do it. . . ." Victory let the sentence trail off.

"Where're your menfolk?" someone asked.

"In jail 'cause they're Quakers, and they wouldn't serve in Constable Gilly's official search party."

"Poor kids," Victory heard one man say. "Imagine them girls trying to do barn work."

"We're beholden to you all who helped us," Faith cried. "Thank you from the bottom of our hearts."

There was more talk, but now that the barn was gone, the excitement was over, and the curiosity seekers drifted back to their wagons and buggies and left. When they were all gone, Gilly turned to Boom. Only the original search party remained.

"We'd best git on with what we comed ta do, Bull. We've wasted enough time on this here tarnation fire. What does yah want ta look at first?"

Bull Boom looked down at Gilly and said, "Send dis mob home, all 'cept Weed 'n three good men with guns 'n hounds."

"Yah men, off home with yah." Gilly turned and cried out. "You're finished fur today. Ifn I needs yah tomorrow, I'll send da same message again."

"Hope my barn hasn't burned down while I've been wasting this day searching," Victory heard one of the men mutter as he turned to go.

When they all had left; Gilly, Weed, Boom, and the three men, all with their hounds and guns, walked away and talked. Then Gilly came over to the twins.

"Now, girls, we comed here ta search dis here farm, but dat barn done put us off. Ifn dose Pettybone slaves was in dere, dey's in hades now. But we's a'gonna leave dese three guards 'n dey'r hounds here, 'n we be back in de morning." He wheeled and gave some instructions to the guards. Boom dangled a shoe and some clothes before the local hounds' noses, and then he, Weed, and Gilly mounted and left. Boom's hounds ran free before his horse.

As soon as the men were out of sight, Victory and Faith went up to Momma, locking the back door behind them. She still slept her troubled sleep. "Let's go back outside, Victory," Faith said. They went out into the barnyard. The three guards stood in a row, still watching the barn, their hounds leashed to Blueboy's wire. The twins stayed in the shadows well behind them. "What happened, Victory?" Faith whispered.

"The cows burned," Victory choked.

"But how did it start?" Victory didn't dare speak there, so Faith led her back into the house to the sewing room, where they could watch the guards and the smouldering ruins from the window and talk at the same time.

"I started it." She looked at her twin, but Faith just smiled, not surprised. "I didn't know what to do. I was so worried about you. I kept looking out the attic windows hoping I'd see you, but instead I saw the mob coming down the pike, torches and all, and I knew they were coming here to search, I just knew it for sure. And you remember what Skinhead said about anyone searching the farm." She quivered. "But it's no good, Faith. The cows burned up, the barn burned up, and they're coming back *tomorrow to search anyway!*" Victory put her forehead against the cool windowpane, and all the tears that she'd been holding in came in a flood.

"Let's go up to bed, Victory. The cows may be dead, but the Pettybone slaves are alive and safe in Canada."

"Oh." Victory looked at her sister. "I'm so selfish I never even asked you about. . . ."

"Tomorrow," Faith said, and pushed her twin up the stairs.

Chapter 26

Tomorrow!

Faith and Victory woke to the muffled crowing of the cocks, still penned up in the washhouse. Faith fixed breakfast, while Victory tended Momma. She gave her the green medicine, two glasses of juice, and then got her out of bed while she washed and dried her, then changed the bed. The sheets were barely wet this morning. The doctor's salve was working, and Momma hardly scratched as she sat in the chair and watched Victory.

Faith came in with Momma's breakfast on a tray, and Victory got her settled back in bed ready to eat it, a pillow across her lap, her Bible beside her. "Just call, Momma, when you're done," Victory said as she bundled up the soiled linen and followed Faith down the stairs. Breakfast was ready, but Victory unbolted the back door and dropped the laundry in the corner on top of yesterday's pile. Where were the washtubs? Absently she scratched her shoulder as she looked about the cluttered barnyard. Well, she'd find them later.

She and Faith had kept the dogs in the kitchen away

from the guards' hounds. But the animals in the wash-house needed to be fed. Victory did that before she washed at the pump and went in to eat with Faith. As soon as they were finished, they put hot coffee, cream and sugar, and some fried cakes on a tray and took it out to the guards.

"Thank yah, miss." They tipped their hats and smiled. Victory and Faith returned to the kitchen, poured coffee for themselves, sat down and were about to tell each other about yesterday when the dogs began to bark. Then the hounds outside took up the barking. The twins ran out the door and looked up the pike. A small band of horsemen rode swiftly toward the lane. Gilly, Weed, Boom, and his leashed bloodhounds, Father, Homer, Peter—and Skinhead! They all rode into the chaotic barnyard.

"Yah guards watch da Strawbridges," Gilly ordered. The men got their rifles and motioned Father and the boys to sit against the shed. Gilly pulled a piece of paper from his pocket and waved it in Father's face. "A search warrant, Strawbridge, all legal 'n proper." He let the paper flutter to the ground before Father's face.

Then Bull Boom took over. He dangled a shoe and some of the runaways' clothing before the noses of the hounds again, then let them loose. The dogs bounded off in all directions, but they found nothing. After last night, there could be no trail left in the trampled yards and barnyard about the house and buildings. Boom finally called them back, leashed them and said, "We search house."

Gilly, Weed, Skinhead, Boom and his hounds went through the house, searching room by room. The twins followed them. When they came to Momma's room, Victory blocked the door, saying, "She's too sick to be disturbed," but Gilly merely shoved her aside.

"Constable Gilly, just what are you doing in my bedroom at this hour of the morning?" Momma sounded like her old self.

"Nothin' Mrs. Strawbridge, 'xcuse me," and he started to back out, but Boom had pushed past him and the dogs sniffed everywhere.

Momma sat straight up in bed and demanded, "Where's your search warrant?"

"Yur husband's gots it."

"Where's my husband?" Momma asked.

"Outside," Gilly muttered and motioned Boom to get out of the room, fast.

The twins began to follow them again, but Momma called, "Faith, I want you." Faith hesitated, but went back to Momma's room. Victory went on trailing the hunters who searched the house from attic to cellar. The dogs had lost interest and ceased to bark since there was no smell for them to follow.

When they came out onto the back porch, Boom said to Gilly, "No good."

"I knows, but we gots lots more ta look at. Dis here farm gots hundurds a acres 'n dem Pettybones could be anywheres," Skinhead said.

"Den why don't de dogs get de scent?" Boom asked.

"Let 'em run free again, maybe dey'll pick it up dis time," Gilly suggested anxiously. Boom shook his head no. Instead they searched all the buildings, then went into the cornfield behind the shed, through the pastures and into the pine forest, finally coming back through the vegetable garden.

"Go now," Boom said. "You wrong, Gilly. My slaves not here." He mounted his horse in disgust and thundered down the lane, his leashed hounds bounding beside him. Gilly gave the Strawbridge men a vicious look, then signaled the guards to come, and all the others mounted and followed in the dust of the angry Boom.

Father leaped to his feet, embraced Victory and asked, "Your mother . . . Faith . . . ?"

"All fine, Father. Faith's with Momma now."

"The Pettybones?"

"Gone. Faith led them away, and I stayed."

"Are they safe?" Homer asked.

"I don't know, but I think they are. Faith and I haven't had a chance to talk. . . ." Father left them, running between the wagons and scattered tools to the back porch and inside. The dogs came bounding out as Father left the kitchen door open.

"How'd the barn burn?" Peter asked, walking over and staring at the smoking ruin. Homer put his arm about Victory and looked into her face.

"Come on, Peter. I'm starving. Let's go in and talk over some hot coffee and food," Homer said, sensing that Victory couldn't speak without crying.

When they went in, Faith was already putting out the breakfast and had mugs ready for their coffee. As she poured the steaming brew into the mugs and handed them to her brothers, she asked, "Did they torture you?" Homer and Peter both laughed.

"Torture?" Peter said. "Almost wish they had. It was the dullest, most crowded, uncomfortable day and night I've ever spent."

"Crowded?" Faith asked.

"We weren't the only Quakers arrested. Mr. Lodge and his three boys and Obadiah Hughes and his two boys were already there when we got thrown in. Didn't have anything to eat except bread and water the whole time," Peter said.

Just then Father came down, and they all sat around the breakfast table. They prayed silently. Homer and Peter began to eat at once, but Father took his coffee cup in his big hands, leaned back in his chair, and said, "Victory, begin."

Homer stopped eating and reached down and squeezed her hand.

Victory swallowed hard, then said, "After you left, we didn't know what to do. But we figured we couldn't do anything with those guards watching us, so we had to get rid of them first."

"What'd you do?" Homer asked.

"We unburied your medicine, Homer, and got them drunk as skunks, and they slept all day until the search party came."

Homer and Peter howled with laughter, and even Father smiled. "Good thinking. Go on, Victory," he said.

"Then Skinhead came and—"

"Skinhead!" Homer's roar lifted him right out of his chair. "That louse was here and—"

"Sit down, brother." Faith tugged at his arm. "Wait until you've heard it all."

Victory told how she recognized Skinhead's voice from the night before, their doubts about him until he told them enough details about the Liberty Well and the Pettybones to convince them that he wasn't faking—then his plan. "Once Skinhead left, Faith dressed up in Peter's clothes, I packed food, and she went into the shed, and that's the last I saw of her until the barn was on fire. But during the day I. . . ." and she told of the longest, most terrible day of her life except for the day Homer had been shot. She didn't leave out a single detail. When she was done, Father leaned back, pulled at his beard, then turned to Faith.

"It's your turn."

"I led the slaves to the Cratty's shack like Skinhead told me. Cozetta was supposed to lead them to Smuggler's Cove where her daddy was waiting. He was one of the guard boats Gilly let out of the harbor to look for bodies or for any boat heading north," Faith explained.

"But Cozetta said she was too scared to take the slaves by herself, and she begged and begged me to go with her. So I made her put on boy's clothes so no one would recognize us. Soon as she did, we set off.

"Cozetta said it was three miles to Smuggler's Cove. Some men and hounds were down along the beach looking in those caves in the cliffs, and we could hear the hounds yelping. We ran like deer down that faint path through the woods. The slaves were so scared they were out of sight ahead of us, and Cozetta and I couldn't keep up. But every time the trail divided, we found them waiting. Cozetta knew the way, and I was so tired from running that I didn't pay enough attention to the forks we took. When Cozetta and I finally got to the cove, Mr. Cratty had the slaves already hidden and the sails up. Cozetta slid down and climbed aboard, and that boat took off east toward Conneaut. I lost sight of it pretty quick.

154

"I started back along the path, never thinking I wouldn't be able to make all the right turns, but I got lost. I got awfully hungry and I don't know where all I went before I came on the river, followed it to Cratty's place and then on home. By the time I got here it was real dark, the barn was on fire, and all those men were trying to put it out. I hid in the pines and finally climbed in that window where we first saw Skinhead, and that's when Victory saw me. And she's told you the rest except that we carried on like a couple of witless females to put everybody off."

"Witless females!" Peter exclaimed. "Don't sound witless to me."

"Remember it wasn't our idea, it was Skinhead's. . . ."

"Humpty Dumpty—a double agent," Homer said. "Guess that proves he didn't shoot me, doesn't it, Father?"

"I knew he hadn't from the beginning, but I couldn't tell you. He's the most useful, courageous man we have working for the Railroad." He turned to his daughters. "The Lord was with you both yesterday. The Pettybone slaves're free—one in death—four in Canada, and poor Heaton most likely gave his life for his beliefs. But because of you two girls, our station's still a secret, and we're still workers to carry out the Lord's will."

Father got up. "I'm going to take a good look at that heap out there." They all followed him. As they stood viewing the ruins, Father put his arms about Victory's and Faith's shoulders.

"Two sons couldn't have done any better than my twins did yesterday."

Chapter 27

Three weeks had passed after the Pettybone escape when Paul vanished.

Victory hadn't been at the breakfast table the morning his chair was empty, for the itch on her shoulder the night of the fire was jumbo fever. Homer told her what happened.

"Father got right up from the table, went to Paul's room, and came back a few minutes later. I expected him to jump on Gretchen Girl right then and chase Paul the way he did the last time, but instead he just sat down and went on eating.

" 'Paul's gone,' he finally said. 'Most likely taken off for California again to find Joshua. I'm not trailing him. He's made his bed; he can lie in it.' "

"And that's all he said?" Victory asked.

"Yes."

"What'd Momma say?"

"Nothing."

"Father's too busy building that barn to go after Paul," Victory concluded.

"I don't think so," Homer answered. "You could be

right, but something's gone out of Father since Gilly put a watch on the farm, and the consensus of the other Underground people was to take the cave off the route. I don't think any of us realized just how much Father lived for this station until that happened."

"But he couldn't continue," Victory said. "A watched station puts the whole line in jeopardy. Besides the other stations are carrying on, aren't they?"

"Sure," Homer said. "Everything's back to normal since the Heaton boat and body were washed ashore. Boom and his bloodhounds went back to MarbleHall, all the posters came down, and the stories in the papers stopped—normal for everyone except us."

"But being put off the Railroad now doesn't mean that it's forever, does it?"

"Of course not, but Father's awfully gloomy. Funny thing, Victory. He doesn't seem to be as sad about losing the barn as he does about the useless cave and that dead jockey and Heaton."

"But those deaths weren't his fault." Victory reared up and fell back again, so itchy that she jerked at the cords that held her. "That happened before the shipment got to his 'divinely protected' station."

"We all know that, but *he* doesn't seem to see it. It's a good thing he has the barn to build because it'll help take his mind off the fact that he didn't get *all* the Pettybones. . . ."

"Thought everyone had forgotten about the Pettybones," Faith said as she came in with a vase of flowers. She put the vase down in the vacant place on the mantel where Victory's diary box used to sit.

"Father hasn't," Homer said.

"I know." Faith sat down and fanned herself with her handkerchief. "And I haven't either. You know what? I forgot to tell you this about the Pettybones, but when I was leading them over to Cozetta's that day, one of the big men said he was going to come back and get his wife as soon as he got to Canada and made some money. And he kept looking around and asked the name of the river, our code name, all those things."

"I've heard lots of them say that, but I've never seen one actually do it," Homer said. "And I don't think Father has either."

"All I know is that's what that big groom said." Faith got up and adjusted the flowers and went out.

"Wonder if Faith brought those flowers for you or for the doctor?" Homer laughed. "Momma said at breakfast he was coming to see you this afternoon."

"Doctor Simmons," Victory said. "Such a gentleman, so handsome that he's got all the young ladies in the county after him—including Faith. And he has all that evidence about us being in the Underground Railroad business, yet we don't know if he's done anything with it or not. Then there's Skinhead—ugly, dirty, sneaky—pretending to be one person yet underneath he's really someone else. You just can't tell about people can you, Homer?"

"People wear masks, Victory. It's hard to see behind them sometimes—impossible in some cases."

"You mean you wear a mask, Homer—and that I do . . . ?"

"Sure. But horses don't, and that's why I love them so. Already I can tell that Nugget's the smartest filly foal we've got. She's training up faster than any of the other foals."

"Oh." Victory almost wept as she looked at the cords that held her. "Why did I have to get this dreadful itch right now when. . . ?"

"There's plenty of time for you to do lots of the training." Homer got up. "You're getting well a lot faster than Momma, so you'll be out there with me sooner than you think. Got to go, sis. Nugget's waiting."

Victory stared out the window at the blue summer sky. These last two months—the doctor, Skinhead, Homer, the Pettybones, slavery, the barn, Paul—she felt a thousand and thirteen years old. Rubbing her back against the soggy sheet, she tried to stop the itching. But nothing would stop it except time. And she had lots and lots of that ahead of her.

She smiled in spite of herself. Nugget—her Nugget —the smartest filly in the whole bunch of foals. Wait until she told Doctor Simmons.